Immortal Embrace

Charlotte D. Blackwell

World Castle Publishing
http://www.worldcastlepubliching.com

World Castle Publishing
Pensacola, Florida

Copyright © Charlotte Blackwell 2011
ISBN: 9781937085476
Library of Congress Catalogue Number 2011930722

First Edition World Castle Publishing July 1, 2011
http://www.worldcastlepublishing.com

Cover Artist: Karen Fuller
Editor: Marissa Dobson

Dedication

To my wonderful family, my husband James, you have always believed in me even when other didn't, thank you for all your support and encouragement. My children Jorden, Shawnee and Lucas I could have never finished this book without your understanding. Jorden you are an amazing young woman and thank you so much for always helping with the other kids when mommy needed to work. You kids inspire me to follow my dreams and never give up. My best friend Kathi, thank you for always being my sounding board and kicking me when I needed it when began to doubt myself. You make me laugh and cry and always there to entertain me. Together we will make them "SKIP". I love you all more then you could know and each one of you has helped me to succeed.

An extra special thanks to my publisher Karen, I can't thank you enough for believing in me and my story, I hope to make you proud. My editor Marissa thanks for challenging me and helping me to see when I could do better. I think we did it!

And last but not least, thanks to all the vampire lovers out there who like me just can't get enough. I hope you enjoy the Embrace series.

Charlotte Blackwell

Introduction

In Greek Mythology it is believed that humans originally had four arms and legs and two faces on one head. The God Zeus was scared of the power these humans had and split them in half, resulting in two humans. He condemned humans to walk the earth searching for their other half to complete them. This is referred to as soul mates, through reincarnation some soul mates may spend many life times either searching for one another or together.

Charlotte Blackwell

Chapter One
Changes

Her scream rips through the entire house, as the family runs to the horrific source, the wailing cuts right through to my very core. The memories flood me of the day I used to bellow the same cry so many years earlier. But I can't think about my own terror anymore, I have a new life now. I can't allow her to go through what I did. What has he done? I know her terror, her fear, the panic that is starting to set in for a girl who has become like a sister to me.

"She's in Caspian's room!" I shout.

Within moments of the painful cry, my entire family reaches the door. Elijah grabs for the brass doorknob, only to find it locked. He pounds at the solid oak door, his demands for it to open becoming more and more desperate as her cries fall silent. I take notice as Elijah and Florence share a glance and then, with his unnatural strength, he throws his shoulder into the door with all his might. The door splinters into pieces as what is left of it crashes to the ground.

Inside the room, Caspian is frantically fighting to save the woman he loves. "I...I didn't... I didn't mean to! I didn't...Please help her! Please!" The tears stream down his face; blood no longer pours from the wound he inflicted on Ashley.

I look at the two of them and wonder *how did this ever happen?* She lays limp in his arms, as he is desperately trying to give her life again. The bed beneath them is stained crimson with her blood. I notice the small puncture mark on his wrist. It is seeping slowly, almost completely closed over. *Surely that is from his attempt to save her. Surely...*

"Ashley, NO! Please wake up. I can't lose you, my love. I am so sorry," Caspian cries in utter anguish.

Isaac and Constance push through the rest of us, to their aid. If anyone can save her, it will be one of them.

"She is too far gone," Isaac observes. "There is nothing any of us can do to save her now."

"Can I help? There has got to be something one of us can do."

"No, Sophia. I'm sorry, but she has lost too much blood, and her heart has stopped. He drank too much too quickly. I'd try to give her blood if I thought it would help, but it won't do any good. I am sorry," Isaac says, "but Ashley is dead. We cannot help her now." His grim confirmation ends all hope.

Every instinct within me tells me to run and cradle her, to use every power within me to breathe life back into her limp body. "I can feel it now. She is gone forever." I didn't need him to tell me; I had felt it the second he released her hand.

"I have much more experience than you, Sophia. In time you too, will have the ability to detect separate entities and feel when the life force leaves," He adds before he rises from his knees and pulls Caspian from her body. "We have all made mistakes, and I'm so sorry. We all loved her."

Elijah wraps Caspian in a bathrobe and leads him out of the room away from the rest of us. Leaving us all standing there for a moment, shocked into silence by the tragic loss.

Caspian has lost the woman he loved, but we all lost a woman we considered part of our family. It is not very often we let someone in, but our Ashley is just...well, she is special or at least was.

"What are we going to do now?" I ask. Glancing around the usually immaculate room, I see it is in total disarray. The white, satin sheets appear black from the dried blood they are now soaked in. Blood splatter covers every wall, as well as the two lovers' clothing that is haphazardly strewn about the floor.

Isaac calmly observes our surroundings and tries to piece together the details. "Elijah will handle this. He is a very wise man, and he will assist Caspian in dealing with his loss and the details of the accident."

Constance agrees. "We will know more after Caspian clarifies what happened."

Constance's and Florence's footsteps pound in my head as they walk down the staircase toward the kitchen. The sound of splashing water echoes through the corridor as they prepare a bucket to do the cleaning. We have to remove any and all evidence of this tragedy.

I realize my senses are increasing from the blood exposure, and quickly turn my focus back to Caspian. "Why wasn't anyone aware of Caspian and Ashley's situation? Could no one sense what was happening? This could have been prevented." My face burns with anger, and my throat is as dry as charred forest. As I become more aware of my surroundings, the drying blood brings the repulsive metallic scent of death. "I better open a window," I say, needing relief. "It is starting to smell in here." It is time to air it out a little; even if nothing will remove the smell of Ashley's spilled blood. I head to the large window at the front of the room. I pull the shades and open the window before taking a seat on the window bench.

Alexander opens a second window on the side of the room. "Agreed. I hate the smell once the blood stops moving and what is left begins to settle."

I cannot help but wonder how the blood can be so appealing until it starts to congeal in the body and reek. The wind rushes in through the open glass, and the scent of her young blood swirls around the room. I can feel the urge hastening through my body. I am ready to come apart.

"Sophia, relax. You can handle this. Nothing is going to happen. We will all be fine."

Alexander understands me only the way a twin can. He is so protective of me, and the connection between us is strong, almost unbreakable. *Why though, brother weren't you watching over Caspian instead?* I thought but dare not say.

With his large hands on my tiny shoulders, looking directly in to my eyes, into my very core in the way only he can, Alexander interrupts my worries once again. "Because he asked me to butt out tonight, Sophia. They had a special evening planned, and he did not want my intrusion."

"I am not blaming you. I am only wondering if there was anything we could have done." I run both hands through my hair, loosening the layers to fall around my face piece by piece. I let out a huge sigh, not wanting to lay blame on anyone. This is just one of the risks we take with our lifestyle, nothing more than a terrible unfortunate mishap.

"What about now? Do you know what happened, what is happening?" I ask, still looking up at my brother, who towers nearly a foot over my diminutive five-four frame.

He lowers his head, letting the sandy blond hair cover his face.

I try to gauge his emotions. I can tell he knows something, but getting him to share it with me is an unattainable feat, at least for tonight.

"Okay, everyone grab a cloth and start cleaning. Caspian doesn't need to walk back in on this mess," Florence urges in her motherly tone as she enters the room with a cache of washcloths and cleaning supplies.

Everyone works together to try to remove the hideous evidence from Caspian's room. This is going to destroy him. He loves her more than anything else, and he will need our help to cope.

◆ ◆ ◆

"He's gone! I had no chance of stopping him. He was exasperated over the accident, and he returned his day ring to me and said he is no longer fit to be a member of our family. And then, just like that, he took off. I...I don't think he is coming back—not ever." Elijah gently places his arm around Florence's shoulders. "Not only has our family lost Ashley tonight, but we're losing Caspian too. We can mourn our losses tomorrow, but tonight we must take care of business."

We all agree and get to work. We never question Elijah; he is the head of this family and demands respect. What reason would we have to doubt him? He never steers us wrong and always guides us in the right direction.

Elijah and Isaac wrap Ashley's body, already growing cold, in a sheet.

"We will dispose of the body," Elijah says, lowering his head at the thought. "The rest of you should continue cleaning the room."

Once again, we find ourselves drowning in silence as the older men in the family remove the body of our friend.

Constance sets the scene in Caspian's room to create the appearance of him running away with Ashley. She even initiates a goodbye letter on his computer.

I can hear Florence on the phone with Ashley's family: "Have you seen or heard from Caspian? We found his room in disarray tonight and a letter on his computer. He said he could not handle the pressure of college and was leaving."

The plan is being set into motion, much like a story being written. We will file a missing person report after the required forty-eight hours. As for tonight, we will pretend to go search for the two lovers that we know are forever lost to us and to each other.

♦ ♦ ♦

With every passing day, I wonder about Caspian's safety and his emotional state. We have not heard a word from him since Ashley died, and my only hope is that he will return to us soon. If or when he decides to, he will know how to locate us. I still cannot believe everyone in town believes our tale that Caspian and Ashley ran away together, but our secrets have been well kept. I only wish they were still with us.

I don't want to leave, but it is time to move on, as we are needed elsewhere. I grab my suitcase, pack my belongings, and prepare for our relocation. All the while, I cannot help being slightly frustrated that Alexander still won't share what he knows. Maybe one day I will get it out of him, but for now, only unanswered questions linger in my mind.

♦ ♦ ♦

It has been almost thirty years and eight moves since I last spoke to my oldest brother on the night when his girlfriend was accidentally taken from us. Still, I am convinced I have seen him lurking in the shadows from time to time, possibly to check up on us. I hope he decides to confront us someday soon. I think about him and the accident every day, that night changed me forever. The ache

12

in my heart returns often, and I miss my brother. He was always willing to tell me what others refused to. Things were much more exciting with him around; humdrumness has taken over since he left...at least until recently, when she came.

Our family is not the same without him; we have since taken in a new girl. She is young, with a birth age of only fifteen. I remember when Constance found her outside the hospital one evening last summer. We knew by the nature of her injuries that she would soon be one of us. We took her in and helped her through the embrace, training her and inviting her into our family.

"It is time to move on again and introduce Danika back into society. Where better to start than the same place we all began our lives again so many years ago?" Elijah declares, and he begins arranging for our relocation.

"This scares me," I confess. "She is still so young. How do you know she won't rebel?"

"Sophia, my dear, you made it through, and she will too. You need to have some confidence in her ability to socialize—not to mention that Alexander, Mati, and you will be with her all the way," Florence assures me with far more confidence in the decision to proceed than I have.

I watch with dismay as Elijah takes Caspian's family ring, hanging on a thin gold chain, and places it around Danika's scrawny little neck.

My emotions get the better of me, and I shout, "How can you just give her Caspian's ring?" *Danika is only a teenager, after all.*

With a firm hand and stern voice, Elijah replies, "He has not shown himself in three decades, Sophia. She may use it until we can have one made for her. It will not take long once we return to Wenham."

That was the end of the discussion, for we never question Elijah.

Chapter Two
The Move

I've never imagined happily ever after. Happiness is not in the stars for me. *How can it be?* I ask myself. I saw how it destroyed Caspian. I will not let the same thing happen to me. That is why I try to distance myself from others. Now, after years entertaining and educating myself, working meaningless jobs, I have to return to high school as a spy and babysitter. I guess this will be a true test for Danika, but I am not interested in watching her every move and all the questions that come with being the new kid in town. Flopping back on my bed, I try to imagine what it would be like if I was normal, if I was mortal.

The past week has been spent unpacking. Moving is a big job, and we are taking the time to set up our house and make it our home. Walking around the house, I feel a sense of belonging, but it is overwhelming to return to the town where everything changed, where we learned a new way to survive. The memories overwhelm me with a variety of emotions, and the lump in my throat makes it even harder to fight back the tears. Things improved for us because of a few magickal women we had the privilege of befriending, but I fear now that Danika will jeopardize it all...but I guess I should have a little more confidence in her and in our training.

When I am finished preparing my room, I decide to help Alexander and Matilda with theirs.

"Why don't you two ladies enjoy a walk around the grounds while I set up the electronics?" my brother Alexander asks. "Sophia, can I assume you still need yours installed?" Alexander gives me a playful nudge.

"You assume correctly," I reply with a smirk across my face. The two of us leave the room.

◆ ◆ ◆

Matilda and I take solace in our little walk around the grounds, familiarizing ourselves with the area.

Taking a seat on the bench in the back garden, I confess, "I think I may like being back here in Massachusetts. We already have history in Wenham, and I believe it's going to prove to be an interesting place for us to live."

"You're right, Sophia. I remember the last time we were here. This is the place that made everything possible, the place where I became part of this family." A slight twinge of pain flickers in Matilda's eyes as she recalls a time so long ago. "That seems like forever now."

Trying to forget about the bad stuff, we look around and lounge in the overcast weather. We are fortunate to have found this amazing house. It has to be the most beautiful house I've ever seen. It reminds me of an old-style colonial mansion. It is just on the outskirts of town and slightly secluded, and is more than large enough for our entire family, all eight of us. Our family enjoys nice things, but even better than that, we love a good deal. I have to say this is the nicest house we have ever had—and at a price we couldn't beat. We all love it, so even when we move again (as we surely will have to someday), maybe we'll keep the house for future use.

I am excited to be here again. We have been gone for years. I feel comfortable here, as if I belong. When I start to feel this way, the logical part of me takes over my mind, and I start to wonder how long it will last. We never stay in one place for more than a decade, and then it is on to the next town.

"How do you feel about going back to school?" I ask while twirling my long brown hair around my fingers, I confirm. "I was nervous, but I am getting a little excited."

"I think it will be fun. I have been getting a little bored and look forward to challenging myself. I think the curriculum has changed since last time," admits the Barbie doll blonde. In true Matilda fashion, she retouches her lip gloss while admiring herself in a compact mirror, before we wander back to the house.

I spend the rest of the night organizing my school supplies. I pick out a plain outfit in an attempt to fit in, as if they won't realize we are the new kids. Small towns like this have lifers. Most of the kids we will go to school with will have known one another since birth. My biggest concern is Danika. We have been easing her out around town all week, and she has done well. I just have a bad feeling about her—a worrisome feeling the others don't seem to sense. Maybe it is the pessimistic side of me emerging yet again. Either way, I hope we do not draw too much attention. I don't like getting close to people because of what happened to Caspian. I guess I should just relax and see what the day brings.

In the sitting area of my room, that is exactly what I do. I pick up a book on Wenham history. Page after page, I learn more about the town history. This was the first town to break off from Salem in 1643. The first settlers of the area were Agawam Indians, and they later sold the land, though a few Agawam decedents still hold a presence in a nearby tribe. It is rumored that they are indebted to the land and still protect the area and the inhabitants. The next section discusses Wenham citizen Sara Good. During the Salem witch trials of 1692, Sara was hanged for being a witch. I think Constance will be intrigued by this story because of her brush with similar witch trials back in the day. I dog-ear the page; I will share it with her later. There was also a deadly outbreak of small pox in 1776, causing all the town children to be homeschooled. I always love learning about the towns we move to. The last time I was here, I learned very little, so I am glad to have this book. I rest it on my table to read more later. My brain is in historical overload, but I hope to have time to learn more before we are forced to move again...*Oh how I hope we get to stay longer this time.*

Chapter Three
Caspian

Writing in my journal, I start reflecting on the past thirty years without my family. Flipping through the leather-bound pages, I see notes–remembrances and reminders of every encounter I have had trying to protect them. I believe they are unaware of my presence or the presence of danger that surrounds them, hunting them. I miss having meaningful relationships, but I must atone for my mistakes, and this is the best way I know how. My heart still breaks for what I did to Ashley and for what her loss must have done to my family. Regret fills me for leaving them to deal with the aftermath of my actions.

I begin scribing my newest journal entry.

August 26th

They are moving again, back to where it all began. They are not aware of the dangers that lie ahead. I will be busy, and only being able to go out at night makes my job more difficult. In times like this, I wish I had not returned my ring. After coming to terms with Ashley's death, I found them, and now I continue to follow the family I once called my own.

Sophia is extremely observant, and I have had many narrow escapes when it comes to her seeing me. The pain she has suffered on my account hurts me to no end. I hope she will one day learn to let go and find love. Her distrust of the new girl (I believe they call her Danika) is well founded though. This one will cause trouble for the family, just as Sophia suspects. Her new scent is drawing the evil closer, and now that they have returned to Wenham, it is closer than ever before.

Today I watched them move in to the place up the hill. This house is a good choice; they have chosen well. It is a secluded place, slightly out of sight and surrounded by a thick forest. But as much as this is good for them, it can also be a detriment. If others cannot see them, they cannot see others, including this evil thing I am hunting. Sitting in the tall trees today, I was lucky enough to catch a glimpse of Sophia and Matilda in the garden, thanks to the extreme coverage in the forest, and the overcast. I also saw Danika watching them from her room. Her need for acceptance and belonging is what worries me. It makes her an easy target. I will need to keep a close eye on her for a while...and whatever may come for her.

Tonight I will scout the area and re-familiarize myself with the town. And I simply must find something to eat.

I close my journal and tuck it away in a safe place, and I prepare for the night ahead.

Chapter Four
New Beginnings

Today is our first day of school at Wenham High, complete with new books and school supplies and the same old façade. I step out the front door of our home, reluctant to embark on this new adventure. I take in the beauty of the land we have purchased, the deep green hues of the grass and many trees; it is so beautiful I can taste it, like a fresh, ripe melon. The sun is beginning to rise, turning the sky beautiful shades of pink and lavender. Watching as Alexander pulls out of the garage in his pearl-white Cadillac Escalade, I grab my bag that's resting on the porch swing. Matilda and Danika are already in the vehicle, and he stops at the front steps to let me in.

As we drive through town, I see a sign: WELCOME TO WENHAM, MASSACHUSETTS POPULATION 4615. The streets are busy with parents bringing their children to the first day of school and older students stopping to pick up friends on their way. I enjoy the chance to make these observations, for over the years, people's mannerisms have changed drastically. What better way is there to blend in than copying the traits of those I watch?

I turn my attention to my new 'little sister' to get a feel for her state of mind. She appears excited; with an ear to ear grin she twirls the straps of her knapsack around her fingers. She looks about ready to pop right out of her seat. "Are you sure you are ready for this?" I ask.

"Seriously, Sophia, it has been a year already. Aren't you ever going to trust me?" Her snarky tone drives me batty. "I am ready to start the day, to be a high school student. Please do not ruin this experience for me."

"Fair enough. You should enjoy high school, and I will give you the benefit of the doubt. Just don't screw this up for all of us." At least I will have Alexander and Matilda to help keep her in line.

Stepping out of the car I instantly feel hundreds of eyes on us, and I try to ignore the whispers in case of any judgmental remarks about the new family in town. On the contrary, my siblings appear to be enjoying the attention. I am happy being slightly more obscure. I follow my siblings through the school grounds. I will not let all the prying eyes bother me, for I am only here to support Danika and ensure the safety of those around her. People are too trusting these days and should be more aware for their own protection.

We take our time walking to the main office. The school building is picturesque. It looks to be about a century old, made of rustic brick, with a large staircase leads to the front doors. There is well-developed greenery, some kind of ivy, climbing the walls and framing the windows. *So much detail,* I think to myself. *They don't make buildings like this anymore.*

A charming smile beams across my brother's face, and his brown eyes sparkle in the morning light. "Well, kids. Are we ready for this?"

Matilda gives a slight wink of her ocean blue eyes. "Back to the land of the living."

"Let's just get this over with. I hate not knowing what will happen. I hope people will just stay away from me. Why do we even bother?" I grumble.

"You know why, Sophia. It's because of me, though frankly, I don't give a—"

"Danika! I will not tolerate you speaking like that. You will act like civilized human being. As for you, Sophia, if you are not careful with your negative talk, you will be the one that causes Danika to fail. We must keep her calm." Matilda's ocean blue eyes grow darker with her anger.

She is right; it is time for me to lighten up a little bit.

"Come on, Sophia. Try to enjoy yourself, maybe even make a friend or two." Matilda encourages in a calmer voice than a moment ago.

"Who in their right mind would...?" I stop myself without finishing my sentence.

Alexander is mad this time. "Try to be a little more positive and support Danika."

"I'm sorry. I will try not to be so skeptical and miserable."

◆ ◆ ◆

Walking into the building I notice the walls are a pale yellow and lined with blue lockers. To my left is the library, framed with glass walls, as if to invite people in. Inside it are many cubicles and rows of student iMac computers. I am sure I have read most of the books on those shelves, but I look forward to finding the ones I have yet to read.

To my right is the main office. It is very bright, with white walls and large windows so they can observe the happenings outside. Everyone's going about their business. A middle-aged man heading over to the wall covered by small mail slots, one for each staff member or school group; he retrieves his memos for the day. A chest-high counter separates the room on one side from chairs on the other to create a waiting room, of sorts. In the work area, there are several cubicles and four larger offices, I assume for the higher officials of the school. The engraved nameplate on the front counter says Ms. Jennifer Hunt.

A nice-looking woman with a warm, welcoming smile greets us. Her strait blonde hair and blue eyes put Matilda to shame. "You must be the Pierce family. Welcome to Wenham High!"

At that exact moment, everyone in the office stops what they are doing to catch a glimpse.

"It is not very often that a new family moves to town. Most families have been here for generations," she adds.

Alexander smiles back. "Thank you. My name is Alexander, and these are my sisters, Mati, Sophia, and Danika."

As she hands us our class schedules, locker assignments, and school maps, Ms. Hunt smiles again and says, "I trust you will enjoy our little town."

"Thank you," we say as we exit the office.

We stand in the hallway outside the office as the students begin to file in for their first class.

Alexander passes our schedules and information out while announcing everyone's first class. "Mati, you have chemistry. I only ask that you do not blow up the school on our first day. Sophia, you get to enjoy history. That should be easy enough for you."

"Ha ha. Very funny," I say with a hint of sarcasm, still slightly bitter that I have to be here at all.

"Well, Danika and I have English in our respective grades. We can meet at lunch in the cafeteria. Enjoy your day, girls," he snickers.

We part ways and began to look for our locker assignments and classrooms. Alexander helps Danika find her way. This allows him a chance to check up on her without the tension between Danika and me.

I have my head buried in the school map, trying to keep a low profile and avoid the curious whispers around me as I search for my classroom. *I really just wish they would pay no attention to me.* I must keep my cool and avoid bringing attention to myself. Suddenly, I managed to embarrass myself. When I bump into him, my books fly out of my hands. Although I could catch them, I allow them to hit the ground. I need to remember that not everyone has super reflexes, and I want to appear normal. That is when I hear it for the first time: the most beautiful, friendly voice I have ever heard. I don't understand how or why, but his voice changes my mood from the very first syllable he speaks.

"I am so sorry! Are you alright?" the enchanting voice asks, already beginning to retrieve my books off the floor like a true gentleman.

Never have I been so distracted before. As he kneels beside me, I catch a whiff of him. He has the most incredible scent, so perfect I can taste it. He is like a perfectly aged wine, sweet and robust. He is like nothing I have ever smelled before – simply intoxicating. *Maybe Danika is not my biggest concern. I want him more than anything I have ever desired before. I should worry about myself for a while. Will I be able to resist this incredible man? It is almost as though he is perfect for me. It has been years since I have been so tempted, and now with hundreds of eyes burning into me, I am tempted once again. I want to run, to scream, but I can't. What can I possibly do? A long time ago, I made a vow–a pledge to never again follow through with such a temptation. I must remain true and strong, but...but I am so unsure of my ability to do so. He is like a bright candy apple at the state fair. I know I shouldn't, but it is so hard to resist. How long can I resist a temptation such as this?* I take a slow, deep breath–as my heart beats a little faster, but I want to, just so I can intake his amazing scent and enjoy the mouth-watering moment a little longer.

Then I look up. "I am. Thank you, although it was my fault for not paying attention. Please accept my apology. Are you okay?"

"Don't worry about me. Name's Nathanial McCord, but everyone calls me Nate."

As I look up at him holding my books that he's gathered, I realize he is magnificent. This young man is the most amazing creature I have ever come across. He offers his hand to help me off my knees and brushes his finger through his creamy chocolate-brown hair. Each strand falls back in place and reminds me of an expensive French truffle. His eyes are the most beautiful sapphire eyes I have ever seen. I am completely enamored by him, rendered speechless. This tall, athletic, perfectly muscled wonder with beautiful broad shoulders stands in front of me with a puzzled look upon his face.

"Are you sure you are alright? You look slightly out of it. Did you hit your head?"

This is not good. I attempt to talk myself down, but there is so much adrenaline running though me. *Okay, Sophia, just get this over with and move on to class. Forget about him, this could be real trouble. You have worked too hard to throw it all away now.* "Yeah, sorry. Just a lot on my mind. I guess I better get to class." *Mind your manners and don't be rude,* I scold myself. "You said your name is Nate? I'm Sophia Pierce. It's a pleasure to meet you."

"And you as well, Sophia. I can see by your schedule we have first-period history together. May I show you the way? You know...for the protection of the other students?" he jokes while already leading the way with my books still in hand.

His joke relaxes me just enough to smile and follow him to class. "Thanks...and very funny, by the way."

Chapter Five
The Struggle

"This is our class." He hands me my books and introduces me to the teacher before taking his seat.

"Welcome to Wenham, Ms. Pierce," Mr. Wilson, a short, proud, middle-aged man says. "Okay, everyone. Take your seats."

"Thank you," I mumble as I proceed to the only open seat left, beside Nathanial, and politely smile at him. I notice him shooing away anyone else who tried to take the seat next to him.

I can't believe I will have to sit next to him for the entire year. My feelings toward the boy are so conflicting. I want to be near him, but for all the wrong reasons, which makes me want to stay as far away from him as possible. I guess the choice is out of my hands now. He smells so good– deliciously appealing. I will have to figure this out before the inevitable happens and I can no longer resist the temptation.

He smiles back. "This is great, and now we can get to know each other better."

"Yeah, great. You are the first person I have met, aside from Ms. Hunt." I try hard to sound entirely sarcastic, but fate is working against me. *I am just going to have to remain calm and remove these thoughts from my head. I will have to ignore his incredible scent, how he appeals to my every desire. I am so confused, wanting to know him and wanting him to know me, the real me. How is he making me feel this way? I have always been so good at keeping my distance. I have worked very hard to maintain the life I live, and I cannot throw it away over one silly boy!* I think to myself. *I need to stay away from him and keep my distance before I go down faster than the Titanic and take my family with me.*

Mr. Wilson stands in front of the class to address us. "Welcome back, everyone. It is nice to see all of you again, along with a new face who's moved to our town. Sophia, can you tell us a little something about yourself? We have all known one another for years now, and it is a pleasure to have someone new in our midst."

I feel twenty-five pairs of eyes staring at me, awaiting my response. "Um, okay. My name is Sophia Pierce, and my family and I just moved here from British Columbia, Canada. I live with my parents, three siblings, and my aunt and uncle. I enjoy leaning about the history of the towns we move to, and...um, well, I guess that's about it." In the background I hear some of the girls whispering about Nathanial's attentive demeanor toward me. From the information I can collect, Nathanial is well liked, popular, and the object of many girls' affections, though he never seems to return the affection. He is more concerned about getting good grades, football, and the scholarship he is hoping to land to help pay for college. From the whispers I caught they can't help but wonder, what makes the new girl so special?

"Thank you, Sophia. Now, class, let's watch a short film on Stalin, a prominent figure in Soviet history. He ranks as one of the world's worst dictators."

Mr. Wilson starts the movie, grabs his coffee mug, and exits the room. Most of the class visits quietly, talking about their summers, but my thoughts were elsewhere.

I have never met anyone so kind before. He so helpful and polite. Nathanial McCord is a true gentleman and a pleasure to be around. I glace over at his notebook as the movie is playing. He is taking detailed notes, thorough and neat. I can tell he is a good student and eager to help me, the fragile new girl in town. *(That's funny. "Fragile" is possibly the worst adjective to describe anyone in my family.)*

Nathanial notices me reading his notes. "So how long has your family been in town?"

I can't distance myself from him when I get lost in those amazing sapphire eyes. The best I can do is to try to keep my answers basic, while I contemplate the best way to resist him. "We got here last week."

"Have you been able to check out the town? We have some great history here."

"We have been busy unpacking, but I have been reading up on the town history a little."

"If you ever need a tour guide, I would be happy to show you around."

"That's so kind of you. I think I just need to make it through today first. Everyone seems a little...well, intrigued with my family's presence here. I'm not sure if I can handle much more attention." I have a habit of blabbing a little too much when I get nervous.

The bell rings, and the sound reminds me of a banshee's scream. I'll have to get used to the sound clanging away between classes, because the noise is hard on my ultra-sensitive hearing. *Class went by fast, thank God. Now I have an escape! I will be in my next class soon enough, and then can get* my bearings. I survived first period, and what is more important the class survived me.

"Hey, look, Sophia! We have photo shop together next," Nathanial says, crushing my escape plan with his enthusiasm.

I know I must be very careful. How am I going to protect him from me, when he renders me downright incapable of hiding the truth? My day is not starting out very good. Let's hope it gets better before it gets worse...a lot worse. I really need to get a grip on this. I feel like my head is about to explode, and I can just imagine what I must look like to everyone since I tend to over think things, and I am sure it shows. Nathanial seems to be a great guy, and I cannot do anything about being in the same classes. I decide I just have to tolerate it and move on.

◆ ◆ ◆

We partner together in photo shop. I just am not capable of staying away from him, no matter how hard I try. *I need more, I want more, and I want him. How can this be? I have never encountered anyone like him before.* I begin to think that maybe moving to Wenham is not going to be as great as I had hoped. There is something about Nathanial, and I will figure it out.

The teacher sends the class to wander the campus and take pictures using digital cameras. As I look around the exquisite grounds, I notice Nathanial snapping some candid shots of me, and I let out a smirk. "Careful. You don't want to break the camera on the first day."

"No camera breaking here. I am more concerned about a heart breaker," he says, laughing.

We start talking a little more, and he asks all the usual questions. "So you're from Canada? What brings you to Wenham? What does your family do? Do you miss your boyfriend?"

"Wow. What is this, some kind of inquisition? Ask as much as you can in one breath, not allowing me to over think my answers?" I joke.

"Sorry. Just curious."

"No problem." I begin to answer using my well-practiced lines. "We moved from Canada, Whistler, British Columbia because there are too many tourists there and the commute was too far. My father is a lawyer, my uncle and his wife are both doctors, and mother is a homemaker. My brother, two sisters, and I are all students. There's no boyfriend to miss. Besides, who would want to date me anyways?" *Considering it is such a poor choice, a downright bad idea,* I thought to myself. I can tell my final comment threw him off a little.

He whispers under his breath, thinking I won't hear. "Who *wouldn't* want to?"

I am shocked by his comment, but I cannot reveal that I heard him. I pretend to scour the campus for something to photograph. *I cannot let his whispered compliment get to me, and I have to stick to the game plan: finish out the last two years of high school, make sure Danika behaves, move somewhere else, go to college, and fight for what we believe in. I cannot allow him–or anyone else, for that matter–to change the plan. It has worked for my family until now, and there is no use fixing something that isn't broken.* Continuing with the task at hand, photography, I try to forget what he said and peruse the area for the perfect snapshot. I get in a few good shots of Nathanial just as one of his football buddies tries to sneak up behind us.

"Gotcha!" the football friend shouts. "Now I have proof you like the ladies," he jokes as he snaps a picture of Nathanial and me and runs off laughing.

"Don't mind Ben. He's just teasing me. I usually concentrate on my studies more than I do the ladies. The boys all think I need a girl in my life to keep me balanced, but I just never had any interest...at least not until now," he admits sheepishly. "I have never found a girl who interested me quite as much as you. Sophia, I know we just met, but I think you are amazing, interesting, and intriguing. I believe there is more to you than you let on, and I want to know what you are hiding," he says, clearly laying his intentions out on the table for me to process.

Analyzing the situation that has popped up so unexpectedly, I begin to wonder, *How am I going to get myself out of this mess? I can't resist him. I can't get enough of him, and I can tell he feels the same. But I'm sure he'll get over it soon. I am just the new girl, a mystery. When he does forget about me, it will be easier for me to forget about him.*

I'm glad when second period is over. Printing off a picture of Nathanial for myself, and I tuck it in my bag. I'm completely enamored by him, and I wonder what it is about him that is so intoxicating. It scares me. I fear not only for him, but also for myself around him. I know I cannot allow a boy I have only known for two hours to affect me like this. It feels as though I have known him forever, as if we belong together. If I become too close to him, everything could come out, and my darkest secrets will be revealed. I must not allow that to happen. Someone may get hurt. He could get hurt. I have to find a way to keep my distance from him, to find a way to resist the irresistible. That's my new task, and I challenge myself to succeed. I've had enough for one day.

Chapter Six
Sharing

The next two weeks of classes drag by, but Danika is responding rather well. I am grateful to have Alexander in my algebra class, although it is getting old watching all the girls swoon over him as usual. I will admit to my brother's stunning appearance, but enough is enough. Sometimes it turns my stomach.

"Sophia, why do you let what others think bother you so much? You need to learn not to pay attention and just let it all roll off of you."

I hate when Alexander noses into my thoughts like that, and I tell him so. "First off you need to stop doing that. Sometimes my thoughts should be private. I know I am miserable, but this is how I keep my distance from people," I say while gathering my books to get ready for my next class.

With a soft, calm voice Alexander stares right inside me, right to my very core. "I understand why you don't want to get close to anyone. You're afraid that what happened to Caspian will happen to you. But, Sophia, the people here are nice and you need to give them a chance. That Nate guy seems very welcoming, and I know he wants to get to know you better. Start with him. Get to know him and let him know you, even if it's only a tad."

"He frightens me. I have never wanted anything as much as I want him. He does something to me. I can't hide from him. Something about him encourages me to enlighten him to our situation."

"That could be a problem if you are not smart and careful, but why don't you just trust yourself a little? You are stronger than you think."

♦ ♦ ♦

As we walk to our lockers, every girl we pass does a double-take of Alexander. I try not to let this upset me. Alexander is right, and I do need to relax. To some extent, their infatuation is amusing. Most teenage girls think of Alexander as some kind of celebrity, a sweet temptation. He is tall, strong, and built like a rock with a slight five-o'clock shadow around his face. His blond hair matches the sand on a Caribbean beach, which makes his piercing brown eyes stand out. It's an unusual combination, but it works; he is stunning. Nevertheless, he is not available, so they need not bother–though they don't know any better.

I try to remember a time when I let someone from outside the family in. It was Ashley. She was an exceptional woman, although we never did share the family secret with her. She knew we were different, just not how different. Since her passing, I have tried to keep others at a distance, and I have been good at it–until now. Nathanial is different from others. Nathanial appears genuine and truly interested in me. He wants to know everything he can find out about me. I feel his brain working overtime in an attempt to figure me out. There is another reason I must stay away from him: he is special, and I want to keep him safe–safe from harm and safe from me!

When lunch rolls around, Alexander and I find Matilda and Danika in the cafeteria quite easily. No one ever seems interested in joining our table.

I freeze with surprise. "Are you kidding me?" I ask quietly.

Alexander stops and asks, "You okay, sis?"

"It is just Nathanial. I know you said to give him a chance, but I'm still reluctant. He's everywhere. I can't seem to shake him, and I feel like he may be the one to get everything out of me. I want to be near him. I like him, and I want to know him. I just don't trust myself with him, and now he is sitting with the girls." I let out a sigh.

"I still think it's a good idea to get to know him, but be careful, Sophia. You don't want to give in to your temptations. We are here to help you control yourself." Alexander reassures me as we continue to the table where Matilda and Nathanial are sitting, deep in conversation.

Danika appears to be smitten with Nathanial as well and is flirtatiously twisting and twirling her vibrant red hair on her index finger.

We reach the table, and Nathanial stops mid sentence. "Hey, Sophia. I met your sister in Advanced Trig. I hope you don't mind me joining your family for lunch?"

"No, that's fine. We have lots of room, but your teammates over there look a little confused."

I figure I can try being more pleasant and friendly. Nathanial is a good guy, and it might be nice having him around.

Nathanial begins fidgeting with the ketchup bottle that is on the table. "Your sister invited me to join you for lunch. She sure thinks highly of you."

With a slight glare, I look over at Matilda. "Do I dare ask why you think that?"

"Never mind. I don't want you getting an ego," she interrupts and smiles.

I can tell by Matilda's mannerisms that Nathanial is trying to gather as much information about me as possible. Lucky for him, Matilda is overly friendly and spills just enough to keep him interested.

Matilda whispers to me, "I get the feeling he is hard to keep secrets from. He is the type of person everyone wants to confide in."

"Yes, me included. There's just something about him that caught my attention right off. I don't even understand why."

Nathanial is very compelling. After knowing him for only a little under a month, Matilda admits to opening up a little about our family dynamics. "Danika is the newest member to join the family. We are not related by blood. Alexander and I fell in love, and we are accepted as a couple within the family rather than siblings. This is okay since we weren't raised together nor officially adopted."

I am shocked she is revealing so much; I guess I'm not the only one that needs to be careful around him. His ability to relax others and extract information from them is unfathomable, and getting any of us to open up so willingly is an extraordinary feat indeed.

"May I try to explain?" requests Danika.

With complete surprise, Matilda encourages, "It would be wonderful to hear your point of view."

Danika looks for approval from the rest of us as she begins. "Our family was not raised together. We came together later in our lives. We had nowhere to go, and the Pierces took us in. They have raised us ever since. Only Sophia and Alex are related by genetics. From what they have told me, it was evident from day one that Alexander and Matilda belonged together."

Talking about the others and their relationships, I begin feeling a little lonely. I have been alone for so long now. I had stopped believing my soul mate even exists until I met Nathanial. Sitting across the table from his incredible scent, I find myself contemplating the possibility that my soul mate is right here in front of me. I know Matilda has a keen sense about souls and is always searching for someone special for me. She has this gift of seeing inside people's souls and can tell if they belong together. Until now, she has never had any luck finding someone for me. From the look on her face, I can tell she feels differently now. *This cannot be a good thing, no matter how much I want it to be true. There is no way he is the one. Our differences are too much to handle in a relationship. It will never work out, at least not in a good way. He may be right for me, but I am more than wrong for him.* I try to clear these thoughts from my head. I do not want to raise any more questions and should pay attention to the conversation going on around me.

With my siblings near, I decide to throw away my inhabitations and be myself. The five of us goof around. We click really well, laughing and joking around. It makes it easy to forget about the entire school watching us, and I even relax a little. It feels good to loosen up and not be so tense around Nathanial. I am beginning to see myself in a new light with him around. Trying to make normal conversation while still checking up on our new sister, I ask, "How are you enjoying high school so far Danika? Are you making any friends?"

"I really like it here. People are very friendly, and nothing has been too difficult yet."

"That's great to hear. I am always here if you need help with anything." We all understand the subliminal talk, but we don't want Nate catching on. I'm even beginning to relax a little with Danika. Maybe I should give her a chance; she is trying very hard.

The bell rings, signaling the end of lunch period. We gather our belongings and prepare to finish our day. I look over to Alexander, and we silently agree that a sit-down with Danika is in order. It has been a month, and we need to make sure she is handling everything alright. I will try to give her the benefit of doubt. She may be mentally stronger than I ever thought.

Chapter Seven
Dinner

Gathering around the mahogany dining table for our daily meal, I decide to share about the past month of school. "This guy in a few of my classes Nathanial, or Nate as everyone calls him, concerns me. He seems to relax all of us and release our inhibitions. I'll admit I'm extremely attracted to him and can't get his scent out of my head. I am concerned about what he may learn or what I may do because of this somewhat embarrassing infatuation."

"I must agree with Sophia. There is something unusual about him, something alluring and disarming. Although I really like him, he is kind, and Sophia's and his souls match better than any I have seen before," Matilda adds as she pours a ladle full of the blood gazpacho Florence has prepared for dinner into her bowl.

In his traditional fatherly tone, Elijah says, "We should meet this boy then, to ensure the safety of the family."

"There is a football game tomorrow night. He's the quarterback," I announce, slightly blushing.

Elijah grins. "It's settled then. We'll attend the game as a family. What about the rest of you? How has school been working out?"

We all look at Danika, waiting for her response. She is quick to oblige. "I love it there. Oh, Sophia forgot to mention how cute Nathanial is too."

"Seriously? You're thinking about that? You are new to this lifestyle, and we have just begun to integrate you back into society. I think you have bigger concerns than a cute boy." My frustration with Danika's adolescent outlook is quick to take over.

"Oh relax a little, Sophia. I am just a teenager, and I want to enjoy being one while I really am."

Why did we have to welcome her into our family? She just knows how to get under my skin, and I don't trust her. As I eat my dinner, I try to calm myself and avoid jumping across the table to strangle her. I wonder if she deserves more credit than I have been giving her, but I realize I just can't give it to her.

Alexander gives me a little look. "I think Danika has been doing very well. She has not had a difficult time dealing with temptation and she has maintained our cover."

"Thank you, Alexander. It has been difficult at times. I just don't want to disappoint any of you. Sophia already hates me and this family is all I have. Constance could have left me outside the hospital that night to fend for myself or so someone else would claim me. I am happy to have a second chance."

"Danika, I'm sorry. I do not mean for you to think that I hate you, although I understand it may seem that way. I guess I'm just having a hard time letting someone in after losing Caspian and Ashley."

With wide eyes searching for approval, Danika begins to plead, "I understand, but don't you think if I was going to do something to harm this family, Constance would have seen it?"

"She's right. I only saw her as part of our family, ever since the night I found her. I think we all need to regroup as a family unit. This should be a memorable experience for all of us. Being back in Wenham again will bring us closer together." Constance begins to clear the table as Florence brings in dessert.

"Anyone interested in some blood sorbet? I infused the donor bags with citrus to give it a nice twist."

We all dig in. Florence is an amazing chef, and after so many years of having to feed directly from the source, she has come up with many new ways for us to feed.

"Florence how is our blood supply? Should I order more from the Hematology clinic?" Isaac offers.

"No. I think we are alright for human blood, but maybe you boys should get some more animal blood tonight. I like to mix the two so we don't cause a shortage with the blood banks. That could raise suspicions."

I admire Florence so much. She's meant to be a mother, always ensuring things are in order. I smile just thinking about her. "Can I come? I could use a night out hunting."

"Sure. Why don't you help me gather the materials?" Isaac suggests.

Matilda gathers the dessert dishes for the table as the boys and I retreat to Isaac's office.

◆ ◆ ◆

"Okay, Sophia. We need to gather supplies. I need the twelve-gauge needles. The sixteen-gauge are used for humans, but I find that a larger needle allows for faster recovery of the blood with animals," Isaac explains.

"You cannot help but act like a teacher, can you?" I giggle.

"I believe in lifelong learning, and you have already had a longer life than any mortal, so it's time to learn something new."

I smile as I look for the needles. "What next?"

"We need the poly bag, that blood bag that has a little fluid in it. The fluid you see is the anticoagulant, to prevent clotting. We also need the tubing and the cooler. That about covers it."

"I thought you sedated the animals to make it easier?"

"Oh yeah, I almost forgot. We need the tranquilizer gun. Good catch, kid."

"Did you seriously just call me 'kid'?"

Isaac chuckles. "Yep. To me, you are a kid. Now come on and let's hunt."

Alexander and I load the supplies in the back of Elijah's H2 and close the tailgate. I love this Hummer.

Chapter Eight
Accepting

I walk into the school with a smile today. I feel so fresh and renewed after hunting with the boys last night. I can't stop thinking about the amazing hiking trail they took me to. I am always grateful for our nocturnal vision; I can still see the lush trees, the wildflowers, and the streaming waterfall. This place reminds me of British Columbia. I think that was the most beautiful area we have ever lived. When I see the beauty of the world, I sometimes think it is not such a bad thing having to walk it forever. I get to see change and development and meet new people like Nate. I am beginning to see what Matilda sees. *Maybe he is the one.* I am getting excited about the rest of the family meeting him tonight.

"Hey sis, snap out of it. I know what you mean. I love it up there, too, but you are going to run people over if you don't watch where you are going and stop daydreaming," Alexander points out.

"Are my thoughts ever my own?"

"Nope. I could share them with everyone if you want to complain." He grabs me around my waist, right in my ticklish spot, knowing he will get a reaction.

I jump and let out a giggle as I turn and smack him playfully. Danika and Matilda both chuckle as we head to our respective lockers and prepare for the day's classes.

On my way to history class, I see Nathanial. "Hi," I say.

"Hey gorgeous. Can I take your books for you?"

"Thanks, but I can manage. Wanna walk with me though?"

"Of course. Hey, are you coming to the game tonight?"

"Sure am, my entire family's coming too."

"Perfect. I'll look for you," he says while opening the door to our class.

Class is over before I know it. Nathanial walks with me to Spanish, this time grabbing my books for me before I have a chance to stop him.

"Thanks, but isn't that a little old fashioned? Does anyone really carry books for girls anymore? I thought chivalry was dead."

He smirks, "Not when the right girl is involved." He lightly brushes a loose piece of hair from my face. I turn my head inward toward his hand and wrist, enjoying the wonderful scent that emanates from his body. It feels as though an electric shock, a brightly charged lightning bolt, is shooting through my entire body as he touches me. It is like nothing I have ever felt before. I'm sure he can tell by the look on my face that something is up, and I can see the same look on his face. *He feels it too.* So many emotions pass through me in a single moment. I am not sure what to do. The feelings going off within my own walls are beginning to tear them down even more. *How does he do this to me?* While I am elated by the feelings he brings alive in me, I am so nervous and fidgety around him. This is all so new to me, and I don't know whether to fight it or accept it.

"Are you okay? You seem a little cold. I have an extra sweater in my bag if you would like it," he offers.

"No, I'm fine but thank you for offering. It must be the excitement. Believe it or not, this is the first football game I've been to." I laugh, knowing the real reason for my chills.

"Seriously?"

"Yeah. High school sports are not that big in Canada."

"Oh, you're gonna love it. I will make sure of that."

"Sweet! I'm looking forward to it. Thanks for walking me to class. It's nice to have a friend."

"My pleasure. Catch you later," he replies.

I know I should stay away from him, but I just have to get to know him better. What a day this is turning into–my every dream and nightmare all wrapped up in one. Nathanial is incredible, and he has dreams and aspirations. I do not want to cloud those or change them. I need to protect him, to keep him safe and on the road he has chosen. My road will lead away from him eventually. I just hope I can control myself with him until then.

Regardless of all this, I will not let my emotions or insecurities ruin my day. I feel great after last night. It has been a long time since I have enjoyed myself like that and just let loose. Hunting is in our nature, but because of the way we choose to live, the way we have evolved has caused us to remove our primitive nature. Doing so leaves us vulnerable; at least this is my reasoning. I am happy my family has chosen to live as members of society, and I hope that one day, more of our kind can do so as well. As I take my seat in class, I try to clear my thoughts and prepare for my day with a smile on my face.

Chapter Nine
Discovered

Nathanial is already beginning to knock down the walls I have built around myself, so maybe I can be a little friendlier. I don't need to carry around such a chip on my shoulder. At the same time, I still don't want to get too close to anyone, too dangerous, but friendly should be okay. I can try to be less uptight and just be pleasant to those who decide to express an honest interest–to those like Nathanial.

I've been sitting next to a girl named Ebony for the past month. She seems to be friendly. I have been observing her and those around her; she does not appear to have many friends, but she also seems okay with that fact. I don't understand it, but maybe we have more in common than anyone might think. Spanish class is a no-brainer. I have become fluent in many languages. Noticing that Ebony is struggling, I lean closer to her. "Can I offer you some help? I know a few tricks."

She smiles. "Thanks. I have never been good in Spanish."

I don't normally let anyone know how diverse I am, but something draws me to her. I wonder what her story is. We begin to chat a bit during class. It soon becomes evident where she is heading.

"So Nate McCord, huh? He is quite the catch."

"Nice guy. I literally bumped into him the first day and we have a few classes together. He has been showing me around, but it is not like that," I insist.

Inside I know it's not true. I am not sure exactly what I feel for or about Nathanial, but I do know he interests me. I will have to see what happens. For now, I will try to keep him at a reasonable distance without fully closing myself off to him.

"You do know he is a major commodity around here, right? All the girls want him, but he is only interested in football...or at least he was until you came along," she announces.

"What do you mean?" I am a little annoyed with her implications.

"Well, not only is he the hottest guy around, but he's also the best quarterback this town has seen in years, if not ever."

"And your point is?" I ask.

She continues, "Well, every girl in school has been fighting for his attention since grade school, with not one success story."

"Okay. But I still don't get your point," I say, still trying to understand.

"I don't mean to offend you. I'm just explaining that there may be a few jealous girls around here. Nate's focus has been on receiving a football scholarship and having the grades to go with it. He comes from a wonderful family, but like most of the families around here, they work hard for what they have and do not have much left for extras like college. Therefore, that is all he has cared about for years. He doesn't want to be any kind of burden to his family. Since you arrived, Nate has redirected his attention. Everyone seems curious because everyone knew his goal, but the way he follows you around like a lost puppy is kind of throwing a few people off," she explains.

I lower my head, slightly embarrassed–a feeling I don't get often. "I don't know what to say."

"We have never seen Nate so attentive to anyone else before. It's like the opposing team sent you as a distraction." She giggles.

"Nope, it was just my parents. No one has anything to worry about. I can't imagine us being anything more than friends," I insist and I start to loosen up again and joke back.

I realize that Ebony is not trying to insult me. She is just warning me. It is nice to gain the new and valuable information about Nathanial as well.

"Well, just take it easy on him. Our football team needs him, and he has never had a girlfriend before," she tells me, almost as if she knows just how bad it would be for me to get close to him.

At that exact moment, she notices my necklace, an heirloom of sorts. "My God!" she gasps.

Reluctantly I ask her, "What's wrong?"

"That necklace. Where did you get it?" She quivers.

"It has been in my family for almost a century. Why?" *How could she know anything about it?* I wonder. My necklace is white gold wrapping around my day crystal, or black diamond which is shaped as a heart as if the gold is embracing the gem in a hug. It is one of a kind; Alexander made it for me before we had it blessed. The witch that blessed the stones gave them to Alexander to prepare in the useable jewelry for us prior to her ceremony. He is a very talented artisan.

"I have seen it before, a picture of it. Grams told me about it. I just thought it was a story. I never thought it actually existed."

I watch as she takes a deep breath, awaiting my explanation. "It is nothing really–just an old family treasure." *I try to calm her, but it's not working; she knows the truth. How? I don't understand.* I have to think of something, but I can't, and I start to panic.

What am I going to do? This girl I met only a few weeks ago knows something is up. How do I explain it to her without letting the cat out of the bag? This cannot be happening. Why me? Why not Alexander? He is much better prepared to handle a situation like this than I am. I have to think fast. How could Ebony have seen pictures of our stones before, and how did her Grams know the story behind it? We are in the right area. Could her Grams be...? Then I realize it's true. "Wait a second. Is your Grams Ms. Edwina?" I ask quietly.

"Yes!" Ebony replies, completely shocked. "How do you know?" she asks.

I pause for a moment and blurt out, "My grandmother told me stories of this young girl she knew and her mother too. They resided in the area back in the day. I know my father has been hoping to contact her."

Although it is partially a lie and I am sure she is aware of it, her eyes say it all. *Ebony knows, and our secret is out!* We both let out a small gasp and stare at one another for a few moments.

"I think I am okay. Are you? Maybe our families should get together and talk later. You have nothing to worry about," I say softly.

"I know. Grams explained that, but I just never believed it was true. I just thought they were stories of an old woman." Ebony shakes her head in disbelief, sending her long black hair swaying from side to side.

"After the football game tonight we can meet at your Gram's house. Does she still live nearby, in that same manor she moved into when she married?" I ask. We have been there to visit over the years when passing though.

"Let's do it tomorrow. Enjoy the football game tonight. I need some time to think all this through. And yes, Grams still lives at the manor. We all do. Will your whole family join us? How many are there?" she asks.

"There are eight of us, four teens and four adults," I reply.

"That's different from the stories I heard. Grams said five adults and three teens, although I also remember one left. Is that about right?" she asks.

"Yes. Our family dynamics have slightly changed, but we will explain that tomorrow."

I remember Ms. Edwina is the granddaughter of the witch that 'blessed' our gemstones, making life, as we know it, possible. If her Grams is a witch, then so is Ebony. "Are you about sixteen years old?" I ask her.

"Yes. I just turned sixteen a few weeks ago."

This means she is coming of age. Sixteen is the age when a young witch realizes their powers. That must be what Ebony meant by 'changes'. This revelation means she knows our secret as well as us knowing hers. I wonder if she knows what is happening to her. This is something I am not prepared to deal with. Inside I am terrified that someone at the school in this town knows our secret already. It is only our first month here, and it is already out or at least suspected. We may need to move already. On the other hand, Ebony may honor her family legacy. My head feels as though it is about to explode, but I have to keep it cool.

We both sit in class quietly and just listen to the lecture the teacher is giving. I know I am in shock and have to assume Ebony is too. I actually want to run out of class at this very moment and talk to Alexander and Matilda. Part of me wonders if I should try to get her alone and take care of this problem and make sure no one ever finds out the truth. As much as I would like to handle things the old way, I can't. I must remain true. I hope that because of who her family is, everything will work out for the best.

I wish Alexander were closer so he could put my fears at ease. Instead, I find myself trying to gauge Ebony's reaction. She seems to be okay. I notice her doodling on her notebook, the same symbol over and over again. I know that symbol and recognize it from somewhere, but I do not recall from where. It must have been something I saw years earlier.

Once the bell rings I say, "Ebony I'll see you tomorrow. I will have Elijah call your Grams." I gather my books and run out of class. I need to speak with my siblings...NOW! Sixth period is cancelled due to the pep rally in the gym to get everyone geared up for tonight's football game. This break will give me the opportunity to meet up with Alexander, Matilda, and Danika so I can fill them in on what just happened.

I find them within moments.

"What's wrong? What happened?" Matilda asks. She can always tell when I am the least bit upset.

Alexander lets a small gasp sneak out; he already knows what's worrying me. Today I am grateful for Alexander's unique gift, for it is actually better than just a gift. He enters others' thoughts, reads them, and interjects his own thoughts. He can also connect whomever he wants to these thoughts, and within a certain radius, he can see into every corner of a person's mind. Right now, he's looking into mine. With Alexander around, we can communicate telepathically without saying anything aloud. It is very cool and useful gift at times like this. Anyone can do this with him, even though most people would not understand what is going on and would just think it's some kind of odd daydream. Alexander is very good at controlling who he connects to his telepathic web.

As all the excited and noisy students are herding into the gymnasium, we Pierce children stand in a closed circle, having a conversation no one else can hear. Alexander controls our thoughts tightly so that no one else can intercept. I explain the events that came about in Spanish class–all about Ebony being Ms. Edwina's granddaughter.

"I think we all realize that she knows way too much. This could become very dangerous to our family. We all agree with the way you handled things," Alexander comforts.

Matilda adds, "Now we just need to stay calm. Everything will be fine. She is from a good family and they have been our friends for generations."

"Is this not the family we need to see about getting me a day crystal?" Danika questions.

"Yes it is. Now we will just have to see them sooner than we originally planned." I put my arm around Danika's shoulder. Now is not the time for grudges, for we need to remain a solid family unit. I can see the shock on my siblings' faces as we head toward the pep rally, somewhat at ease that we at least have a plan.

Although we all agree to stay calm and that there is probably nothing to worry about, we are concerned, but we each try not to let the others see. We're all scared she may share this with her friends. She promised to keep it quiet, but until we see it with our own eyes, we can't be sure.

Just around the corner from the gym doors, I spot Ebony. "That's her." I watch as she appears to be backed against a locker.

Then she shouts, "I told you to leave me alone! You know nothing about my family."

I prepare to intervene, but there is no need. The blonde-haired girl falls over backwards, and about a dozen lockers fly open, sending a shower of papers and pencils spewing every which way.

Chapter Ten
Ebony

Walking out of class with my head low, I try to process the information I just received. *Is everything Grams told me true? If that is Sophia in the picture with Grams as a child, then it's true that vampires exist, and if they do exist, that means Grams is a... a witch. What does this mean for me? Am I a witch too?* As I get to my locker and begin to put my books away, I have so many questions. I just wish this day would end. *Soon enough,* I tell myself.

"Hey, witch girl! Why don't you hop on your broomstick and fly away?" a voice shouts.

I glance up; it is that awful cheerleader, Mel. She is always trying to get under my skin—and today of all days. "Mel, just leave me be. You know nothing about my family."

"I know what you are. My family has history here too, you know."

Trying to forget about her, I feel a crowd of emotions raging within me. *Why did our friendship have to end? We were always so close, until high school.* I can't understand what happened to change everything, but nothing seems to change things back to the way they were.

"What are you going to do now, witch? Put a hex on me?" she jokes.

Keeping my head slightly down, I look her in the eyes. "I did nothing to you, Mel. Can't you just leave me and my family alone?"

"You mean you did nothing *yet*. I know about your family and all they can do."

"I told you to leave me alone! You know nothing about my family." I feel as if I am about to boil over. In an attempt to calm myself, I turn back to my locker and try to forget about Mel and her unfounded accusations.

Out of nowhere, she pushes me, and I fall against my open locker. Slowly picking myself up, I turn and look Mel in the eyes. I focus every emotion within me on her, and the anger takes over. Every locker around me flies open, and she blows over backwards. A tingling overcomes my body as I wonder, *What the hell just happened?* Dozens of spectators stand there, watching every move I make. A few girls help her to her feet.

"Ebony, come with me!" a familiar voice calls.

"Matt, I—"

"No, not now and not here. Let me get you out of here."

I feel comfort in his hand as he leads me away. Walking past Sophia and her siblings, I give a pleading look. "What's happening to me?"

Sophia reaches her hand out to me. "Tomorrow."

♦ ♦ ♦

I'm lucky to have someone like Matt in my life. He does not pass judgment on anyone. Last year when he moved here, I didn't feel so lonely anymore, because he befriended me.

"Are you okay now?" he asks while wrapping his jacket around my shoulders.

"I...I...I don't understand."

"You will but until then, I am here for you."

58

"Thank you."

"Let me drive you home. Forget about the pep rally today."

"I think you are right. I am sorry, but I think it's best if I skip the game tonight as well."

"No problem. Would you like me to stay with you?"

"That is not a good idea. I think I just need to be alone. Please go enjoy the game."

Tonight I want to call a family meeting. I need to tell Grams everything about Sophia and her family and this episode with Mel. Grams will know what to do.

Chapter Eleven
Concern

I look over at my siblings, shocked at what we've just witnessed. "Can you believe that?"

Danika is stunned. "What exactly was that?"

"You just witnessed what can happen to a supernatural being when emotions get too strong. This is why we worry about you. Ebony is just coming of age, learning of her powers as a witch. She is obviously telekinetic, meaning she can move things with her mind," Alexander explains.

"Okay. Well, the pep rally is about to begin. We can talk about this more at home," I insist.

As we enter the gymnasium, a voice booms over the loudspeaker. "And here they are the newest members of our school. Please help me welcome the Pierce family, Mati, Sophia, Danika, and Alexander." The entire school population starts applauding and cheering to welcome us.

Although I do not like being in the spotlight, I feel very welcomed, and there are no more judgmental whispers. Now there is nothing but warm, welcoming cheers. *Is this what it will be like here? Are the people of Wenham really happy to have us join their community? This could truly become home— something no place has ever been before.*

Nathanial sneaks up behind me and whispers, "Welcome" as he grabs my waist to tickle me.

I giggle and smile at him. He is doing it again. He has this way of breaking through my wall, but I know I have to figure out a way to keep him away.

"Come on! You can sit with the team since you and your siblings seem to be the guests of honor." He hurries us to our seats and joins in the rally.

I really don't know if I will be able to keep away from him–or anyone here for that matter. I am beginning to enjoy it here, perhaps a little too much. The last thing I want to do is let my guard down. There are too many loved ones at stake if I do.

Nathanial is called to the stage, and I begin to cheer as though we have been going steady for years. Not only do I shock myself with my whooping and hollering, I shock my siblings too. *What in the world am I doing? What am I thinking? This is not the way to keep him at bay.* The pep rally was a ton of fun but now that it is over and everyone is dispersing, we decide to go home and fill in the other members of our family on the possibly life-changing events of the day.

◆ ◆ ◆

We explain everything about Ebony and my encounter with her.

"We knew Ms. Edwina's granddaughter attended Wenham High, but we thought we had a little more time before you'd run into her. I saw her in a premonition," Constance explains.

I remember Constance telling me about her visions. She sees the future, but she doesn't always know when the things she envisions will happen. She also does not share everything she sees; she is protective of us and does not want us to worry needlessly. She shares only what she feels is important to our well-being. Constance once told me that she believes things left to fate work out for the best. It is more normal that way.

"I still cannot believe that Ebony openly used her powers like that, right there in the school hallway," Matilda adds.

I look around at each family member. "From what she told me, this is all very new to her. She may not know how to control them yet."

"Although you made arrangements for tomorrow, I will call Ms. Edwina tonight and ensure that all is okay for our visit. She may want us to come by sooner rather than later." Elijah heads toward the study to make his call, while the rest of us continue talking. We confirm the details of our meeting tomorrow.

After he's off the phone it is clear Elijah is excited to see his old friend Ms. Edwina and to finally meet the granddaughters he has heard so much about. "She is concerned but said Ebony has retired for the evening. She says tomorrow will be better for her." He can sense the tension we all have. "Kids, you need not worry. This is a good family. We would not be who we are today without them," he assures us.

We trust him explicitly, but we are still concerned about the day's events. He can tell how uncomfortable we "kids" are with the situation and it annoys him slightly.

"Kids, I do not want you to worry about this. You know what a long-standing history we have with Ms. Edwina. Her family will not do anything to harm us or to reveal our secrets. Everything is safe with their family. We knew this would happen when we came back here. As for Ebony, we will help her through this transition. So please try to have a good time tonight," Elijah strongly insists. "You will see when we meet with them. You have known their family as long as I have and you know it will be fine."

"Okay. But what do you suggest I do about this young man Nathanial? Should I not worry about him either?" I question.

"That I am not sure about. We will have to meet him, but you will have to be careful around him, as he sounds very compelling," Elijah adds.

"Sophia, we would not have come here if I had sensed anything that might endanger our secrets," Constance reassures.

I do feel better after talking with the family, and Elijah told the truth. We have known Ms. Edwina forever, and she and her family have earned our trust. I know I am panicking for no reason. As for Nathanial, I will just have to wait and see how everything pans out with him. It will be no easy task to resist his incredible appeal, but I think I have enough confidence in myself.

♦ ♦ ♦

It is time to start getting ready for the game. It's getting a little chilly tonight, and I agree to allow Matilda to help me get ready. I would normally dress down with my hair in a ponytail and my vanity glasses on, but as hard as I try, I cannot fight the feeling Nathanial is giving me. I have to be myself and leave the loner façade behind; I want to look nice for a change. Matilda picks out some nice jeans, a fitted top, and a three-quarter-sleeve button-up sweater with an oversized belt. It's not too far off from what I would have picked, aside from the fact that she dresses me head to toe in designer labels. I would have put on my UGG's, but she insisted on a pair of Jimmy Choo knee-high boots. It is nice, albeit flashier than I prefer, but then again I did tell her I want to look nice and she is accomplishing that.

"Let's keep your hair down, the way you love." Matilda begins to straighten the long brown layers that look as if they've been kissed by the sun.

Matilda has a gift when it comes to fashion. "I can't believe how good you are at this, Mati. You have the layers framing my face perfectly. I love it. Thank you." I wonder if Nathanial will even recognize me.

"You are most welcome. You know I love doing it."

When we are all ready, we head to the game. I can't believe how nervous I am, as if I were a real schoolgirl with a crush on a boy. Two out of three ain't bad, I guess.

"You are a real schoolgirl – just one stuck in time. Congrats. You have accomplished every woman's dream."

"Alexander, if you plan on reading my thoughts, you can at least drop the sarcasm."

Chapter Twelve
Dedication

At the game, we score some great seats in the first few rows at centerfield, right behind the home team bench. We all enjoy football; it is a great contact sport. The excitement of attending my first high school game is building up in me, or maybe it's just the excitement of seeing Nathanial again. We join the crowd as they jump to their feet and cheer while the team runs on the field, ripping through a big paper banner the cheerleaders have made for them with markers and poster paints. The entire team is hungry for the first win of the season, and the excited and screaming crowd is pumping the energy they need right their way. Nathanial leads the team to centerfield, and once again, he astounds me.

Feeling a dull poke in my side, I turn to find Danika elbowing me. "What?"

"He's looking through the crowd for you. God I wish it were me he was looking for."

Ignoring her later statement I look up at him, and then, out of nowhere, he stops and drops his helmet right in front of me. His mouth is hanging open like a Saint Bernard staring at a steak. I don't know how else to react so I just smile and wave, as my heart nearly leaps out of my chest.

He smiles back and mouths, *"This one is for you, gorgeous!"*

I can hear him breathing the words ever so softly above the crowd's cheers. Keeping him at a distance is going to be harder than I ever expected. I am experiencing feelings I have never had before. I feel giddy about Nathanial's reaction to me tonight and excited to watch him do what he is so passionate about, what he loves. I have such a feeling of confidence and pride, and it seems Wenham is giving me a sense of security that I haven't felt in decades. I even feel like it may be okay to let Nathanial in, at least a little. That way, I can keep an eye on him and make sure he remains safe. I am overly protective of him, even though I cannot explain it. *Can it be true? Could he be the one? We only met last month. Is that what they mean about love at first sight? About finding your soul mate? No, it couldn't be. I do not want him to be a part of this. I want nothing more for him than a long and happy life, free from danger, secrets, and drama. Why does he confuse me so much? I have never experienced such conflict within myself before.*

Constance whispers, "It's meant to be, my dear. If you fight it, things will just be worse. This is what he wants as well."

Once again, Alexander shares my thoughts with the others. "How can *he* want this? He does not even know what *this* is!" I reply.

"He will," she confirms.

"I see it, too, Sophia. Your souls match perfectly, like no match I have ever seen before" Matilda adds.

I sigh and turn to watch the game, but in spite of all the action on the field, the sidelines and in the stands, I mostly watch Nathanial. I can't help wondering if my family could be right, if Nathanial really is my soul mate. *Are we meant to be together?* I just can't understand how he could ever want this. I would not wish this kind of existence on anyone–and that's all it is...an existence and not any kind of life.

"The game is going great," Isaac observes.

Everyone is excited as the halftime whistle blows. The halftime show begins, and in the backdrop behind the band and the cheerleaders, the bright orange numbers on the scoreboard shows that our team is up by fourteen points.

"Wow! Those cheerleaders are really good," Alexander says with a sadistic smile.

"Are you kidding me?" Matilda smacks him upside the head.

We all chuckle and Alexander jokes, "Come on, darling. We have been together over a hundred years, and you still get jealous. How cute."

"My love, there is a difference between jealous and annoyed," she smirks. "It is a thin line of course, but it may be a line you want to avoid walking on."

Florence shakes her head. "I don't know about you two, but can we please just enjoy the rest of the game?"

In less than an hour, the game ends, and our team is victorious by thirty points. This is just what Wenham High needs for its morale.

"I can't believe Nathanial made five touchdowns! He was on fire tonight!" I exclaim, bursting with unbridled excitement and pride.

The entire crowd starts chanting his name, "Nate! Nate! Nate is great!" as the other players parade him around on their shoulders. The local newspapers are snapping pictures and preparing for interviews.

I am so happy for him and the team. He looks even better than he usually does, if that is even possible. Nathanial is so happy and excited, and his eyes are sparkling with joy. I never imagined they could shine so brightly, but as he looks at me, his eyes light up like bright blue shooting stars dancing across the sky. I stand next to my family as we all watch this magnificent man who is hailed a hero by his teammates and the onlookers. *But I can't let him in, and this is going to be one of the hardest things I have ever faced.*

"And we will all be here with you, sis." Alexander wraps his arm around my shoulder.

The team parades in front of us. Nathanial pats the shoulders of his teammates to put him down. I watch as he pushes his way through the crowd and runs up to me. He wraps his arms around my waist and swings me around. I melt into his strong sweaty arms.

When he finally places my feet ever so gently back on the ground he kisses my forehead and with his index finger lifts my chin up ever so slightly so I am looking right at him, right into him, and he into me. "You are my lucky charm, you know. Now I can never let you go." He smiles.

"I doubt that," I reply.

"I gotta hit the showers. Will you wait for me?"

"I wish I could but I have plans with my family tonight, and they're kinda important. I'm so sorry, Nathanial. I wish I could help celebrate your victory." I pout, knowing once again I am not being fully honest. We need to be clear headed for tomorrow, so I do not want to cloud myself with Nathanial.

"No worries gorgeous. It won't be the same without you there, but maybe we can catch up on Monday," he suggests.

"Until Monday then...and congrats. You were amazing out there tonight."

"Aw, it was nothing. I was just showing off for a pretty girl." We both chuckle, and he gives me another hug and runs off to the dressing room to take of his pads.

This is it. Every time I see him, I let him in a little more. I can't fight it much longer. Maybe Wenham is the wrong place for us. I am starting to wonder if we should leave and find another place to settle for a few years. I truly don't want to hurt Nathanial, but it seems like no matter what I do, he's bound to face some pain on account of me.

There I go again, flipping back and forth with my emotions. I wish I could just decide what to do and stick with it. He just has me feeling so many new things that I don't know if I am coming or going. I can't wait for this day to be over. Maybe I will be able to clear my head. I just need to be alone and think, maybe read a little. That always helps me when I'm at a crossroad.

"Sophia, we all know you are worried about this boy, but we all agree he is okay. I have never encountered such good in a person in all my years. You have nothing to worry about, and everything will work out. Do not be afraid to let him in a little. He may like what he finds, and you may as well," Constance tries to reassure me.

I decide to try to relax about the situation a little. A few more things to deal with and then the day will come to its end.

It's just so hard. After knowing Nathanial for only a few short weeks, I cannot get this boy out of my head. He is truly incredible, and that's why I think I need to keep him at a distance. Nathanial McCord is intended to do great things, and he'll never find those things if he is tied down to me.

"Sophia, you are the most incredibly insecure immortal I know. Most hold their head high and have such confidence but not our little delicate Sophia, always worrying and concerned about others," Alexander states.

"I am not delicate! I just cannot understand why anyone would want to be friends with someone like me. It is better to keep others at a distance. That way no one can get hurt!" I yell. I close my eyes for a short moment and collect myself; I am able to calm myself easily. "Don't worry about me anyway. There are more important things to deal with right now. You can hire me a shrink later." I joke, trying to lighten the somber mood I've brought upon everyone.

"She's right. We have things to deal with now and we can talk about this later," Florence says.

I'm grateful we are the only ones left in the stadium and others can't hear our conversation over the celebrating cheers echoing from the parking lot. The last thing we need are stories floating around the grapevine.

◆ ◆ ◆

Once we leave the stadium and get in the car the excitement of seeing Ms. Edwina rises in me. It is almost palpable. It has been a long time and it is more than overdue. We agree that maybe we should have contacted her and her family when we first decided to move back to the area. I reminisce of our time with Ms. Edwina, one of the most intriguing women I have ever known. She is more understanding, knowledgeable, and caring than anyone in the world. If Ebony turns out to be half the woman her Grams is, she will make it very far in this life.

Danika says, "I don't understand why or how our family is such good friends with a witch. I thought you said vampires don't get along with other supernatural beings."

"Ms. Edwina is different. Her family has always been allies with vampires of our kind–the ones that choose to live civilly and not bring harm to the mortals," Florence explains.

It's not really that we don't get along with supernatural's, it's just many believe they are the superior race.

Elijah adds, "She is very old fashioned. She always knows where we are and always sends us Christmas and birthday cards. We enjoy having someone to keep in touch with, and all of us send her letters throughout the year. We are aware of the difficulties of her life, but we do not truly understand the struggles she has faced. This will give us the chance to catch up and reminisce as well."

I already like Ebony, even if I worry too much. Therefore it will be nice to meet the rest of her family and deal with all our secrets out in the open. I hope Ebony is as understanding as her Grams. It would be so nice to have someone at school that I could trust with the truth. For so long, it has seemed like my family against the world. Now maybe, just maybe we will have a confidante.

Chapter Thirteen
Answers

We take the fifteen-minute drive to the most charming old manor. I notice the old oak tree out front; I think the manor is at least a century old. The beauty and history of this home is breathtaking. Ms. Edwina and Ebony are on the front porch, awaiting our arrival. Everything is just as I remember it, and I find it amazing that the manor has stayed in the family for so many years.

We exit our cars and head up the walkway. Ms. Edwina is wearing the most welcoming smile, and Ebony seems very relaxed as well. Seeing the two women together puts my concerns at ease. I wonder what Ms. Edwina has said to the girls thus far.

"Hello, Ms. Edwina. It is a pleasure to see you again. You are looking well." Elijah greets her with a hug. Even though Elijah said she looks well, to me she seems fragile and weakened by her many years.

"Not as well as you, young man. Why, you have not aged a day," she jokes, and we all giggle as she adds, "It is good to see you, my old friends. It has been far too long. Please come in," she offers, opening the door for us.

"Thank you," we say in unison.

Following the two women through the large oak door, we take a seat in the family room of their lovely home. It is just as I remember it from years ago. I notice the fireplace mantel filled with pictures taken throughout the years. I notice a picture of our family with a young Ms. Edwina alongside of the family pictures she has.

"I would like to formally introduce you to my granddaughters, Ebony and Eliza. These girls are my pride and joy," Ms. Edwina announces.

We enjoy catching up over tea and biscuits that Eliza brought out for us. One of the benefits of a day crystal, it helps us digest human food, in order to fit in better.

"Well, we have been moving around every few years, enjoying the many sights the world has to offer. As I mentioned in my letters, Caspian left the family about thirty years ago. Although I would like to introduce you to the newest member of our family, this is Danika," Elijah introduces.

"It is a pleasure to meet you Danika. You are very lucky to have found such a family."

Danika smiles as she looks around the room. "Yes, I am lucky...only I didn't find them. They found me."

"Oh? I'm sorry. Would you mind sharing the story with us?" Ms. Edwina requests.

Constance stands. "I would love to share." We nod, and she continues. "Last summer, when I was leaving work after a late shift at the hospital, I found Danika in the back alley to the rear of the institution. I was ready to rush her into the emergency room when I noticed the nature of her injuries. There was a vampire bite mark on her neck, and I noted dried blood around her mouth. It was obvious that a vampire had embraced her and then left her to fend for herself. I had two choices. I could have destroyed her then or bring her home to join the family. Danika was so young, just a little girl. I could not destroy her, so I did what had to be done. I brought her home with me. Once I arrived the family agreed with my decision, and we began to train her. Danika has more determination than I have seen in years, and we felt it was time to introduce her back into society."

Ms. Edwina examines the new member. "I can see you have done a good job with her, and I assume she is in need a crystal."

"You assume correctly. She is using Caspian's for now, but one of her own would be appreciated," answers Florence with a smile.

"Then my dear, we shall bless one for you before the evening is complete," she says, casting a friendly smile toward Danika.

"Shall we get back to the girls for a moment? They really seem to be lovely young women. Ms. Edwina, I must say it appears that you have done a wonderful job raising them alone." Elijah walks around the room, looking at the many pictures.

"Yes, they are magnificent, though I may need your assistance explaining this to them. Ebony is just coming of age, and she was more than a little shocked to realize all my stories are true when she saw Sophia's necklace. She was also quite terrified by the incident at school yesterday." Ms. Edwina looks toward Ebony with pain and concern.

"Of course. It would be our pleasure. You know we will always be here to help your family. You are the ones that gave us a fighting chance when fate did not allow it," Elijah says.

I find it nice to hear the stories Ms. Edwina shares with us. There is one particularly sad story, the one of her daughter and son-in-law, the girls' parents. She had written us about the tragedy, but it is different to hear her tell the story herself. I don't think she has told the girls the entire story yet, as she mentioned needing help to explain things.

"After Ebony was born and it was known that a new pair of 'Magnificent Ones' were here, it became very dangerous. Eden, the girls' mother, swore to protect them from harm as any mother would. Normally a witch can show signs of their powers right from birth, but they are not aware until they come of age. Eden decided to hide the girls' powers until that time, and this would conceal any signs of their magnificent powers. A very powerful demon came to attack, one that only the power of Magnificent Ones could destroy. He killed Eden and the girls' father, before I was able to assist. She had put a protection spell on the girls until they both gained powers. She completed it just before her death. I was not able to extinguish the demon's powers and he swore to return one day. I do worry about the girls, and I need help to prepare them for that day," Ms. Edwina explains.

I can tell by the girls' reaction that this is the first time they have heard the whole story. They appear surprised and a little frightened. They have always believed their parents had died during a break-in. They don't understand their own power and why their mother and father had to die to protect them.

"Because Ebony is coming of age now, both girls are beginning to receive their powers. The power-hiding spell is now releasing. They have a few questions and I have many fears that the demon will return now since he can probably sense their powers like a beacon in the night," she continues.

"May I try to explain?" requests Florence.

Everyone is in agreement. Ebony and her sister take a seat and quietly await the explanation.

"Girls, as you know by now, you are decedents of Salem witches. Most people falsely believed them to be evil because they did not understand the amazing powers they possessed. When a descendent of those witches comes of age, they start to realize their own powers, which they inherit from their ancestors. This usually occurs around the age of sixteen, and the change from mortal to witch begins."

"Is that what has been happening to us, this coming of age? I just thought we were going crazy." Ebony admits.

"Yes, my dear. I did not know how to explain it properly to you girls, so I have just been waiting for you to come to me with your questions," Ms. Edwina confesses.

"That's okay, Grams. You gave us hints with all your stories about the witches. We understand that you might have been concerned about how we might find out," Eliza comforts.

Florence continues, "Your powers will increase in strength as you learn to control them. You are beginning to recognize these powers. You have always possessed them, but until you were old enough to use them properly, the powers remained weak, and normally only an experienced witch could recognize them within you. Because of the spell your mother used on you, not even an experienced witch could see them. Your powers were completely hidden from all until recently. Once you master one power, it sometimes releases another power within you. A well-trained witch can possess many different powers," Florence informs the girls. "The Salem witches you are direct decedents of were the most powerful of their kind. Like them, you will be protectors, fighting for the greater good and protecting innocents from evil. Within the witch community, you girls will be like celebrities or heroes, and everyone will know who you are. It is truly an honor, and it should prove to be very exciting. Are you following me so far?" she asks.

"Yes. Please continue," Ebony responds, slightly shocked. "Please go on," she requests again.

Florence smiles. "Of course. It would be my pleasure. You sisters are the 'Magnificent Ones,' a pair or more of witch siblings born from the most powerful witches of our time. There are a few like you throughout the world, and they are always born on the sixth of the month at the stroke of midnight. Your ancestors were very strong and foresaw your powers. On your own you are great, but when you combine your powers, the two of you will be unstoppable. Your powers complement each other and can link together to help you use the power of the moon, the power of 'triquetra.' Only witches born into a family of great magickal history on the sixth of the month can match this power. The triquetra power is here for when the universe most needs it. With this power, you can fight evil and possibly save humanity."

"The Salem witches have an amazing history. I recall a time when Salem witches were hanged or burned. The women persecuted were wrongly accused, for Salem witches were too intelligent to be caught, and they kept their secrets well hidden. These are the most powerful witches the world has ever seen. The biggest misconception is that witches are evil, but as in everything, there is a balance–good and evil in this case. A good number of Salem witches worked to protect the innocents, the mortals. Most do not know about all the creatures and dangers of the world, and they believe it all to be fiction, a myth. The majority of it is true to some extent though, and that is why they protect others," Constance adds.

"Wow," Eliza says, trying to take it all in. "How do we know how to use this power or when to use it? And do we know who the other triquetra witches are?"

"Your ancestors left you with a cookbook, of sorts–your own *Book of Shadows*. This is a book of spells, potion recipes, and information on how to destroy certain evils. It lists the various entities your family has encountered, both good and evil. Our family is probably included in this book. The various potions you can make can help you along the way. There is really only one rule and that is that you must not use your power for personal gain. If you do, this could be very detrimental," Florence explains.

"Where does your family fit in to the picture? Aren't vampires evil? Are we supposed to fight you?" Ebony asks, grasping her sister's hand.

"That's easy. Some vampires are evil, but only if they were evil in life. There is a lot of history that explains it, but we were good people in life and try to be in the eternal life as well. I hope you would rather fight with us than against us."

"May I show them our story?" Alexander requests.

"Yes. That is an excellent idea," Elijah says, and we agree.

"Show us?" Eliza asks with a puzzled look on her face.

"Just relax. I can show you everyone's thoughts and memories. It kind of plays out like an old movie, and it may seem as though you are daydreaming. Some vampires have powers, too, and mine is telepathy. Not only can I read others' minds, but I can also share my thoughts and the thoughts of others with whomever I choose. This is our story as I remember it, from right before I became a vampire." Alexander sits back, relaxes, and opens his mind to everyone in the room.

The young witches follow his lead and try to relax as well.

Chapter Fourteen
Alexander's Memories

It was the late nineteenth century in Italy, a warm night on the seventh of August in 1894. Shortly before the witching hour of midnight, I started on my way home from a friend's house. As I walked down the dark street, a woman's scream rang through the deathly silent night. There had been many odd disappearances in the area in the weeks prior, keeping the masses inside after dark. So much fear came through that scream (though the familiarity of it did not yet register in my head), and it chilled me. The urge to help this woman overpowered my own fears. I needed to find her, to help her.

I began running toward the alley in the direction of the scream. On the damp, dark alley floor, I found her beaten, bruised, and bleeding to the point that her loved ones would not have recognized her. She was a young woman–no more than seventeen or eighteen–and she was fallen, broken, and helpless. I ran toward her and placed one of my hands over her neck, where her blood had drained. One of her arms appeared be broken and was contorted in a way that arms should not bend. In an attempt to stabilize it, I carefully held near the largest break with my remaining hand, but I felt her battered bones crumble between my fingers. Looking over the woman as I held her wounds, I noticed the ring on her hand. It reminded me of one my twin sister had received from the Duke. I released her arm and brushed the long mess of brown hair away from her face. I instantly felt every bit of her pain as I realized I was trying to save my own twin sister, Sophia. My heart ballooned into my throat. A feeling of sickness and panic took over.

When my throat cleared, I yelled for help. I held her close. I did not want her to see the absolute panic burning inside of me. Attempting to calm her, I insisted I would help her. I could not lose the person who was closest to me in the entire world. Unsure of how she would ever survive such a cruel attack, I tried to keep her calm and secure, safe and loved in her final moments on Earth.

I began to think of our loved ones and what her passing would mean to them. She was to be married on the weekend. *What is she doing out here?* I knew she had been unhappy about her upcoming nuptials, and I thought maybe she needed to take a breather, a moment for herself. The family was likely wondering where she was at this very moment. I continued to scream for someone to help me, to help her.

Then from out of nowhere, a man came. He was short and thin, and I did not believe he could help carry her, so I begged him to go get help. As he approached us, he walked in a measured, composed pace, as if nothing were wrong. *Could this man move any slower? Doesn't he see and hear that there is a problem?* Then I abruptly became apprehensive, and an uneasy feeling came over me that he was planning to harm me. Sophia's breathing became heavier and more rapid and she appeared slightly panicked. In that exact moment, he pounced on top of me and began biting me and drinking my blood. Several painful moments later, he left us both for dead.

This thing, this monster was what hurt Sophia, ripping her arm apart and crushing every bone in it. He chewed her neck apart as if it were a piece of raw meat. His eyes were a deep crimson red with the darkest black outline around his iris, as if the middle was burning with fire. He was like a vicious wild animal gone mad, with gnashing teeth as sharp as razors. He was a creature like nothing I had ever seen before.

I was terrified for both of us, and I began to realize I would never be able to save my sister...or myself. I began to look for peace, my last comfort, and tried to forget the horror of this monstrous being, but I was not successful.

In an instant, something came over me, and I began seeing everything he saw. I could not explain it, and I did not enjoy it. The visions I began having would not stop, and I couldn't control whose mind I entered or who entered mine. At least we were together in life and in death; it was just my twin sister and me. What disturbed me the most about the visions was that he was only doing it for fun, for pure entertainment, and not for survival. This man–this monster–was the cruelest of masochists.

◆ ◆ ◆

"Would you like to take a break?" Alexander pauses.

Ebony and her sister's eyes are huge as they ponder the same terror Alexander and I experienced in that alley that first fateful night.

"Just let me get some water for everyone," Eliza stammers.

Matilda decides to join her in the kitchen and help. We can hear them discussing the story we are all reliving, "Eliza, if this is too much for you to handle, Alexander can stop.

You can read about it in your *Book of Shadows* rather than relive it as though you were there and it is happening to you," Matilda tries to explain. "It can be too much to bear."

"Thank you. It's hard, but I think we will better understand by experiencing it this way."

Once they return to the family room with a tray of drinks for everyone, Eliza encourages Alexander to finish.

Alexander continues right where he left off.

♦ ♦ ♦

Everything around me was starting to go dark, and I was growing weak. I no longer had the strength to go on, to survive. That is when I heard their voices: two men and two women who told us everything would be okay. "Here...drink this. It will help," one of the females said.

It was thicker than water and had a strange taste, difficult to explain. It was sweet like nectar, so refreshing and so good. As I drank, I began feeling stronger. I opened my eyes to find myself drinking from her wrist, drinking her blood. I looked for my injured sister and saw she was doing the same. I couldn't understand why we were drinking her warm blood, pumped right from her veins, without being mortified at the idea. I couldn't fathom how it could taste so good.

Suddenly the two men grabbed us and carried us away with no effort at all, as if we weighed no more than a feather. They took us back to their cottage to heal and I wondered why they didn't take us to a hospital instead. It did not take long for us to transform and heal, but we did spend several weeks at the cottage, I don't really remember much of our first days there. Little by little, our saviors explained what had happened to us. We learned that their names were Elijah, Florence, Isaac, and Constance, and they were vampires.

They had explained that a rebel vampire (even vampires rebel against their parents) had attacked us. They had been trying to hunt him down and stop him for a while, but they were always just a few moments late. That is how they found us, because they were out looking for him. Constance also had a vision of our special abilities and of us joining their family, so when they found us and realized we were the ones she had seen, they completed the Embrace and began to teach us their ways.

◆ ◆ ◆

"See, some mortals have special qualities they are unaware of," he explains, looking at the girls. "There are also a few who are aware of their abilities. When one with such abilities becomes a vampire, this ability grows and strengthens. For instance, if a person is a good judge of character as a mortal, they might be able to see others' intentions very clearly as an immortal. Does that make sense?"

The two coming-of-age witches nod silently, encouraging him to go on with his tale.

◆ ◆ ◆

Throughout the next few weeks, Elijah and his family provided us with the blood we needed to survive, animal blood, just until our transformation was completed and we could learn to feed ourselves. Our broken bones healed in mere days, and the bruises and cuts were miraculously gone in only a few hours. Everything we needed to stay alive slowed. Our hearts slowed beating, and I noticed we did not need to breathe as much and would sometimes go long periods without taking a breath. We started to lose our appetite for human food and gain an appetite for blood. At this point we don't have our day crystals yet, and to digest human food can be painful, similar to those with lactose intolerance or celiac disease. Thanks to the day crystal your family blessed for us, it is possible to ingest food, although for us it has no nutritional value. Vampires are not dead like most myths believe, we are the undead. We still require the basic necessities to survive; it is just much harder to kill us, because of our healing abilities. And we don't age, so that we can always look good to attract or prey.

Being thirsty was a difficult new experience. A horrible pounding would start in our heads, a burning in our throats, noses, and guts. As our fangs began to emerge, our jaws ached. We became very irritable; I remember feeling as though I could have ripped someone's head off if they so much as glanced at me wrong. This is the best way to describe bloodlust, and why they kept us inside. That way they could teach us to control our thirst and prevent us from harming anyone the way we had been hurt.

♦ ♦ ♦

"We still can get like that now, but we learned very quickly not to let it get to that point. After more than a century, we know how to control our thirst and are usually good at ensuring we do not experience it while we are around mortals. We try to avoid compromising situations that might tempt us to harm anyone to satisfy our needs, but we are occasionally tempted to drink, and in those cases, we have to control our natural urges," Alexander adds to his memory before continuing.

♦ ♦ ♦

Sophia and I began to notice other changes as well. We began sleeping less and less, as we don't require more than a few hours, but there's not much else to do when the sun is out. We began gaining incredible strength and speed, and we became so light on our feet that we could sneak up on each other. That only worked for a short amount of time, though, because we were soon equipped with super hearing. Our amplified hearing could be enough to drive a man insane, and it was one enhanced skill we had to quickly learn to control. We became photosensitive, to the point that the sun would burn us, which was extremely painful. Our physical appearances began to change slightly as well. Our skin lightened to a flawless porcelain shade. We also began to expel extra pheromones that would help attract prey, making us irresistible. Our eyes were a bright red color with a dark ring around the iris. They were not as dark as our attacker's, but they were red nonetheless. This improved when our thirst was controlled, and our eyes returned to their normal color. The only time they turned red again was when our thirst or bloodlust returned.

During the evenings, our new family taught us how to use all our newfound powers and super senses. They taught us how to survive and thrive in our new lives, if you could call them "lives" anymore. We were shown how to improve our reflexes, how we could run faster than anything creature on Earth and not hit a single thing while doing it. We could do almost anything: scale walls, climb, jump great distances, or even swim across the ocean. We learned to use every corner of our minds. Most mortal's use only ten percent, but we use between eighty and hundred percent at any given time. We learned about the power of persuasion, and we became more powerful than anyone could ever imagine.

It may not sound so bad so far, but it is. Really, we are nothing more than monsters with a bloodlust–a need to kill. We are doomed to spend our eternity on Earth, and every day of that eternity, we must fight a war against our own instincts so that we do not harm anyone. We need blood, and we crave the blood of humans. Animal blood will never satisfy us the way human blood does, nor does it keep us as strong. To make matters worse, we can smell the blood pumping through human veins and hear their hearts beating. We can also sense the pulse and the blood flow of animals, but it is just not quite as tantalizing as those of humans. Elijah's clan, or "family," as we call it, taught us that we don't have to be monsters. We can live civilly and be invaluable members to society. We learned how to combine animal and human blood into meals that satisfy us and keep us strong, all without causing harm to humans.

Once we were strong enough, we traveled Europe for a few years, trying to find a place to call home. Our new family continued to teach us every day, and we learned about the six traditions. These are a sort of vampire law that a council of vampires came up with so we could live civilly amongst the mortals. We decided to try North America since that was where Constance saw us settling. Once we arrived in America, we began our search to find a better way of existing, and we ended up in Salem.

It was there that I found Matilda or Mati as we now try to call her. She was being held prisoner, and the mayor at the time believed she was a practicing witch. Although persecution was no longer practiced, he was determined to destroy her. He had done things to her against her will, and she threatened to tell his wife and the town. The vengeful mayor conjured up a story and brought back some planted evidence from the Salem witch trials. The townspeople all turned on her and prepared to burn her at the stake. Constance was convicted in 1899, centuries after the Salem witch trials that took place in 1692, where twenty people were executed by hanging. Many people still believed that witches existed and they were correct. Therefore, they continued to execute anyone who they determined was a witch, and since Mati looked very similar to one of the women who was convicted in 1692, people believed her to be the reincarnated soul. This made the mayor's revenge even easier. They may have been correct about some, but many of the women hanged during the trials were not actually witches.

In an attempt to save herself from a horrible, painful death, she tried to hang herself. She was almost dead, and her mortal body was beyond saving (due to the lack of medical advancements at the time), but I needed her; I knew she was meant for me. When I bit her neck to allow the venom to enter her system, close to her heart, it was the most wonderful thing I had ever tasted. I did not want to stop, but knew I had to if she was going to join us. As difficult as it was, I pulled myself away before draining her of too much blood, and then I bit my own wrist and gave her a drink of my own blood to complete the Embrace. We took her to our settlement to begin her transformation and teachings right away.

After we got Mati to our settlement and trained her, we continued our search for help. This was difficult because we could only go out at night. We began looking for a mystical witch we had heard about. She helped our kind, but she had rules as to whom she would help. We spent years searching for her and finally found her in the 1930's.

About ten years earlier, we had found Caspian. Caspian was eternally twenty-two when we found him, and he had already been a vampire for about 200 years. Caspian told us he was tired of living alone, feeding off any poor soul that crossed his path. He had been trying to live like us, off animals, but he was having trouble and needed support. He joined our family, and we supported him and helped him through the transition.

Caspian did well, but it was difficult at times because he had already tasted so much human blood that it tempted him all the time. The meals Florence prepared helped slightly, but there is no taste like the fresh feed. We kept a close eye on him, knowing he was a member of our family and he had good intentions. He was a good addition to our family because he taught us things and brought a new insight, as only Elijah and Florence were older as vampires. They were both about 350 years old when they found us. Isaac and Constance had joined them about 100 years before us, and they all had something to teach Sophia, Mati, and myself.

The mystical witch we found in the 1930's was Ms. Edwina's mother. We told her and her young daughter, your grandmother, our story. We had passed her test, for we have been surviving on animal blood and donated human blood since 1894, when Sophia and I became vampires–the rest of them even longer. Although we did have a few slip-ups in the beginning with some evil beings, we truly tried our hardest to abstain from all mortals. Caspian was the only exception, as he had only been "pure" for about fifteen years minus the occasional slip-up.

The witch knew this was true because of your Grams, for even as a young girl, she was able to detect honesty. Ms. Edwina did not know it yet, but her mother knew how to tell by the reactions she gave. She was a bit concerned about Caspian but trusted that with our help he could remain pure.

Your great grandmother agreed to help us and provided our family with a mystical gem we wear in our jewelry. It is a rare black diamond called *veneficus lamia sol solis partonus*, which is Latin for "magickal vampire sun protector," but we just call it our "day crystal." Your great grandmother placed a spell on it that allows us protection that not many other vampires have.

◆ ◆ ◆

"That's pretty much it," Alexander says.

"What do the day crystals do for you exactly?" Ebony asks.

"With the protection of the day crystal, we can live similar to mortals. It enables us to walk in the daytime and eat human food without an ill feeling. It also raises our body temperature to something that can seem a bit more normal–still cooler than mortals, but not as cold as ice. Our eyes are not blood-red like those of most vampires, and they remain the original color until we become hungry or smell blood, at which time they will turn red or black, sometimes they can change in accordance to our moods as well. The day crystals also help decrease our cravings for human blood. When we are wearing them, holy water, various herbs and garlic cannot harm us, under normal circumstances these things don't really hurt a vampire, but make them week or ill. Everything the day crystal provides us, keeps us from being detected as easily, though there are some vampire traits that still apply."

"Like what?"

"Well, for starters, we do not age and are immortal. Wooden bullets can slow us down and are harder to heal from than other injuries, but we can be killed with stakes and all the normal things that kill a vampire. Although the best way to destroy a vampire is to behead and burn before the body heals, although if a major life function such as the heart, or brain function cease the vampire will die. We have to be invited into a person's home before we can enter. Also, we have to be cautious and fight the urge to drink human blood, as the day crystal just decreases our cravings, and we still have the need. It is more difficult around open wounds, and it takes a lot of practice. That is why it is so amazing that Isaac and Constance are doctors. They deal with it regularly and are always expose to blood. Anyway, I hope all this helps you understand us a little better," Alexander says.

"Sure does," Ebony says.

"Well girls, that is pretty much our story and how we became involved with your family. We have been living amongst the mortals civilly since about 1935. Your Grams was only about five years old when we first met. She did not know of her gift of honesty until she was older, but mothers always know their children, so her mother knew and could tell as long as Ms. Edwina was in the room. We have remained allies with your family ever since. Although it has been over twenty years since we last saw one another, we have a strong bond and remain in touch through letters," he finishes.

"Wow," says Eliza. "Just...wow."

Chapter Fifteen
Book of Shadows

"I hope you are not too freaked out over this. I think we can all be great friends now that we know the truth about each other," Matilda suggests.

"Yeah. It will be nice to have full disclosure with someone outside of our family," I admit, glancing over at Ebony.

She smiles and replies, "It will be nice to have someone we can trust with our family secrets. I would be up for trying to be friends, as long as you don't like witch blood."

We all begin laughing.

"Nah. It's a little too bitter for my liking," Isaac jokes.

"I was just wondering where Caspian went. You said he left?" Eliza asks.

"Well, that is a whole story of its own, but the condensed version is that he fell in love with a mortal. They became very close and decided to become intimate. Caspian could not control himself, and in the end, he accidentally killed her. It upset him so much that he decided to run away. He gave us his day crystal and left. It all happened about thirty years ago. Last we heard, he was in Inuvik, Canada," Elijah says as he shares a pained glance with Florence.

"Wow. That must have been horrible for all of you." she replies with sympathy.

"It is always difficult to lose a family member, but he lost so much more in her death. We hope to find him and have him rejoin our family one day," Florence admits.

Ms. Edwina rises from her chair and heads to her private office down the hall. When she returns, she is carrying a large leather-bound book. I notice the book has hundreds of pages; all old parchment with some smudged gold edging, and on the cover, there is a triquetra symbol. Both of the girls perk up with excitement when she addresses them. "Girls, now that you are old enough and have some understanding, this belongs to the two of you now. This is your *Book of Shadows*. Anything you may need is in here. If and when you come across something that is not in here, add it for future generations. Study this and learn it, for this book will teach you and give you a few surprises too. You can also learn about those before you, as there is history in these pages, so make sure to add some notes about yourselves as well," Ms. Edwina explains.

"Really? What kind of spells does it have?" Ebony asks.

"Anything you can imagine, my dear. You must always remember though that you must never use any magick to improve your life or make things better, easier, wealthier, or happier for yourselves. That would be considered personal gain or black magick, and being self-serving with your craft can prove very dangerous. You must only use magick to help others."

Ebony releases a smirk from the corner of her mouth. "So I can't use it to deal with that awful girl at school? That really sucks."

In a very stern and intimidating tone, Mrs. Edwina looks at the girls and says, "Ebony Triggs, this is no joking matter.

Can you not understand that magick is serious? I trust you girls, and Wenham needs you."

"I'm sorry, Grams. I was just kidding. I would never do anything to disgrace you like that–even though, that Mel is her own kind of witch most of the time. You and Eliza are all I have. I am serious about receiving this information and great power, and I am ready to help people however I can."

"I am glad to hear that. Now both of you girls come here."

The two girls stand in front of their Grams, ready to receive the power that is rightfully theirs. As they reach for the *Book of Shadows* together, the triquetra symbol in the center of the cover illuminates with a green glow, and when they both touch the book, everyone in the room can see the energy that flows from the tome to each girl.

Almost frozen, we all watch as before our very eyes the most amazing thing happens. Ebony and Eliza both look up to the ceiling, their eyes never leaving the light that radiates from the book. It is similar to the light on top of the Luxor hotel in Las Vegas, albeit on a much smaller scale.

That is when I notice the girls' eyes are almost completely white; they are in a trance of sorts. In that very instance, the light retracts, and the girls drop the book to the floor and fall to their knees around it. The area around them begins filling with their steamy breath, as if they have just stepped outside on the coldest night of winter.

"Are they okay?" Matilda asks.

"Yes, my dear. What you are witnessing is the transfer of power from all the ancestors in our family. The girls are feeling no pain–just a miraculous serge of power and energy. They are now fully connecting as the Magnificent Ones and can begin learning their craft," Ms. Edwina explains in a very soft voice, so as not to interrupt the energy transfer.

Once the girls become lucid and coherent again, we help them to the sofa. They both appear exhausted, and we allow them time to compose themselves. Florence, Constance, Matilda, and I decide to help them to their rooms so they can prepare for bed.

"I'll see you tomorrow, Ebony. If you want to talk, I left my cell number on your nightstand. Call me anytime," I whisper softly.

It has been a long day. We say our goodbyes and excuse ourselves. Our family needs to go scout some animals and prepare for the week ahead by stocking our supply again. Since Isaac brought donated blood home from the clinic yesterday, we should be good on human blood for a while. I can't face the same temptations as that first day. I need to be stronger. But a new sense of relief rushes over me. I am glad to have Ebony to trust, for I was so scared yesterday when she figured it all out. I have never truly trusted anyone outside of my family before, and now I know I might be able to trust others–to let some of them in, if only a little.

Chapter Sixteen
Settling In

Over the next several weeks, my siblings and I continue to settle in to our routine. Ebony and Nathanial both are becoming huge parts of that routine. I am even letting go of the average girl façade, and I am just Sophia. Ebony and I are becoming the best of friends she is amazing. After school and on the weekends, I enjoy helping her work on her powers, spells, and potions. She is telekinetic and is getting better and better at moving things with her mind. Eliza works with her as well. The two sisters, the power of the moon bonded by the triquetra symbol and blood, is shaping up well. They have the power to become the most powerful witches the world has ever seen. They practice with the family *Book of Shadows*, but it must be protected as well because if it falls into the wrong hands, the book could end the world as we know it.

◆ ◆ ◆

I begin to dwell on the biggest problem I face, and that is not being able to stay away from Nathanial. I need to get to know him better, though I still can't understand why I have this constant yearning. Although I have tried to keep my distance, I can't fight it any longer. I simply must be near him. In the back of my mind, though, I always remember how things worked out for Caspian and his lover, Ashley, and I do not want to find myself putting dear Nathanial in that situation. He deserves someone better–someone safer–than me.

Lunchtime arrives, and we hang out with Nathanial and Ebony. Her boyfriend Matt joins us today as well. I really feel the need to talk to Nathanial. He must think I am crazy, always struggling with my feelings for him, which I know are quite obvious. I try to push him away, but every time he utters one word to me with his perfect voice or looks at me with his captivating eyes or even comes near me with that alluring scent, I am sucked right back in to wanting him again.

"Nate, you're a really good guy," I tell him. "I'm trying to keep you at a distance for reasons you might not understand, but I...well, I just can't. What is it about you that makes you so irresistible?" I ask.

"I don't know, but I feel the same way about you. You are someone I want to know, and I want you in my life so bad. Why should we fight it? Look at what you are doing to me...you are turning me into nothing but a big sap. My whole vision of what I want for my life has changed because of you, you know?" he admits.

My thoughts and worries begin to take over again. I don't know what to do. I don't want him to readjust his life because of me, especially because I know there is no future for us and never will be. I will never be able to explain that to him, yet I feel so drawn to him. He really is a wonderful person, and I wonder if I can really trust him enough to tell him everything. *If I could, and he doesn't find me completely insane, maybe we could enjoy a few years together without this tension hanging over us. No, no...it's just not a good idea. Who would ever knowingly want a vampire for his girlfriend? I* remember that Caspian did not even tell Ashley when they were together, and in the end, that did not work out for anyone. "I don't want you to change anything for or because of me, Nate. You don't know what could happen, and it would not be good for either of us," I insist.

"Well, I really think it's too late for backing out now, don't you? We are just going to have to roll with the punches. This is where life is leading us, Sophia, so will you please just stop fighting it already?" Nathanial reaches his hand out to mine.

Lightly touching his fingertips, I answer, "I refuse to promise anything, Nathanial. Your friendship means everything to me."

"Well, that's something, I guess. Now let's just see where that takes us," Nathanial rebuts.

◆ ◆ ◆

After school, I excuse myself to my room. I can't stop thinking about Nathanial. *Maybe he is right and I shouldn't fight it. Maybe we are meant for one another, however long we may have together. I learned from Caspian and his mistakes, and I also have the help and support of my family. I have never found anyone that brings joy to my life the way Nathanial does. Is it possible that I should just enjoy this for as long as I can?*

Nathanial and I become closer every day. I want to tell him everything, but I can't. I need to protect him from the truth. Matilda confirms that he is my soul mate and that he is pure, but I don't need her conformation, because I already know this on my own. He is a more amazing person than I could have ever fathomed could exist. He's even a true gentleman. *What high school guy opens doors and pulls out chairs?* Nathanial has old-fashioned manners, and that's a refreshing changes from the other self-serving, impatient, disrespectful kids that I know in this generation.

I begin thinking about all the things he has shared with me. When I look at him, I just get lost in the sapphire waves of his eyes. With every passing moment, I feel myself giving in to him and letting go of all my inhibitions. I even start to accept that fact and wonder if maybe my fate set out to be as horrible as I originally thought it would be. My mind is turning to mush as I over-think the possibility of a relationship with Nathanial, so I do the only thing I know to do: I call it a night.

♦ ♦ ♦

It is the first of November, a nice overcast day. It's about forty degrees, brisk but not cold, or at least not for me. As I walk to the car, I decide to share with Danika a little, who is turning out to be less of a problem than I first suspected (aside from her obvious crush on Nathanial). "This is my favorite time of year, just before the snow sticks to the ground for the winter. It smells so fresh, like clean fresh linens hung out to dry, or a small babbling brook coming off the snow-capped Rocky Mountains."

"Yeah, you're right, Sophia. It's beautiful, and I must admit I've never noticed the smell of air before." Danika smiles as she takes in a long, deep sniff.

"As you get older, you will notice many things you never did before. You senses are still maturing. The older a vampire is, the easier things come to them. You know...like practice makes perfect." I chuckle at my own cliché.

I'm really beginning to like this town. It is a nice place with lots of history, old buildings that are hundreds of year's old and well-formed family trees. But even with everything I enjoy, I am still trying not to become attached or get too comfortable because I know all too well that it can all change in an instant. It's difficult to avoid making myself at home here, though, especially with such great and welcoming people around.

♦ ♦ ♦

"My older brother Luke is away at college," he tells me. "He received a full-ride scholarship to Harvard. Of course my parents are very proud of him, and I hope to follow his footsteps. My parents always hoped for another baby, but due to complications while delivering me, they couldn't have one," Nathanial says with a sad look on his face that lets me know he blames himself for their heartache.

From everything I have been learning about the McCord family, it seems his parents believe it wasn't in their destiny to have another baby and are happy with the two sons they have. "Your family seems to be just as amazing as you are. From what you have told me, I think your parents are very content with their lives. Do both of your parents work?"

"Yes, and they work hard. My mother is a nurses' aide, and my father works in construction. They do everything they can to provide a dream life to both of us boys. We are very lucky to have them as our parents."

I don't think Nathanial realizes that he and his brother mean everything to their parents; I noticed it the first time I saw the way they looked at him, the night of that first football game of the season. It was our first major outing in Wenham, and even from a distance, I could feel the love they had for him. I have dreamt of love like that. I just never imagined I would ever find it, and now it is sitting right in front of me.

Nathanial explains how his parents save every penny they can for college. This is why receiving a scholarship is so important to him. He does not want to drain their savings, especially since Luke received a full-ride scholarship. Nathanial wants to achieve the same. Family is everything to the McCords, and they are always so thoughtful and considerate of one another's needs and wants. When I was a mortal, I always wanted a family like that, but I guess I can be grateful for the amazing family I have now in my immortal life.

Aside from my big secret, Nathanial and I are getting to know everything about each other. I love learning all the little things and make mental notes of them: His favorite band is Nickelback; his favorite show is *House*; his favorite color is green; his favorite book is *The Da Vinci Code*; and as far as movies go, he adores *Star Wars* almost as much as I adore him.

"You know *Star Wars* is in everything." he adds with a chuckle.

I am starting to learn his little mannerisms, like how when he is confused about something, he bites on his lip and smirks, turning up the left corner of his mouth and showing off his adorable dimple, or the way I often catch him staring at me when he thinks I am not paying attention. Everything about Nathanial is amazing, and it all just makes me want him even more.

With each passing day we grow closer, and nothing can stop it from happening. After more than a century, I am finally allowing myself to fall completely, utterly, and hopelessly in love with someone, with Nathanial. I sometimes forget about my situation and feel like the luckiest girl in the world, if only for a brief moment.

Chapter Seventeen
Letting Go

"So, Sophia, the winter formal is only a few weeks away, and I was hoping you would allow me the privilege of escorting you," Nathanial asks with complete confidence.

"I would be honored," I agree.

"Perfect." He smiles, and we both let out a little chuckle. He excitedly moves closer and hugs me.

At this moment, time seems to slow. We gaze into each other's eyes. As we move slowly toward each other, I can feel his breath and hear his heart racing. I begin to feel weak. I have to be careful, and every instinct I have tells me to turn away, but whatever piece of a heart I have left wants to hold him and never let go. As we move closer, our lips touch ever so softly. Nathanial's arm slowly tightens around my waist, pulling me even closer. This is the most amazing feeling, like millions of fireworks exploding inside my body. The kiss continues with his left hand cupping the back of my head, moving around to my cheek, and stroking along my cheekbone. His right hand is still wrapped around my waist. This kiss is so soft, gentle, but utterly passionate. A crowd starts to form, and everyone is in shock. Nathanial has never been interested in anyone, let alone kissed anyone before.

We don't even notice until Alexander taps Nathanial's shoulder. "Hey, get a room, bro, or else we should start charging admission for this," he jokes.

We part and realize we are in the school courtyard with an audience. As is par for the course for his usual class clown antics, Nathanial turns to the crowd and shouts, "Thank you, thank you! Hope you all enjoyed Act 1. Please tune in next week."

I bury my head in his chest and giggle a little.

"Sophia, sweetie, I am sorry. Are you alright? I shouldn't have disrespected you that way. Please forgive me," he begs.

"I am great–just a little overwhelmed. There is nothing to apologize for," I insist. I wonder if he regrets our kiss and asking me to the dance.

"I should not have showed off like that. It was very disrespectful of me. I feel horrible. You deserve so much better."

"Nate, you have nothing to worry about. I am fine." I give him a small kiss on the cheek, and in usual form, he grabs my books. This time is different, though, because he also grabs my hand, and we walk to history class together. Today, November 26, I am finally hand in hand with the love of my life–a love I never thought existed or that I deserved...and I only met him a few short months ago.

History is more exciting than it has ever been because Nathanial gently holds my hand under the table as we watch a movie about the cold war. I am so glad he is in so many of my classes. This movie is boring, but we are building a history of our own, and I must admit it's an exciting feeling to not have to fight my urges for Nathanial anymore.

After class, as Ebony and I are chatting about today's events, I notice Danika talking to a guy. I don't recognize him, so I ask Ebony who he is.

She takes a good long look at him. "Hmm. He doesn't look familiar, but I don't know everyone. Ever since my magickal incident that day, no one really crosses my path anymore."

"I noticed that too. It must be nice to finally have some peace from all the bantering and teasing," I reply.

"Yeah, they leave me alone now. There're a few people who are curious and kind to me, but I think it's just because they're scared I'll put some kind of hex on them or something." She lets out a laugh. "Come to think of it, that could be kinda fun," she adds.

"It could. Maybe we should look into it," I joke.

"As much as I would love to, I have to avoid personal gain and focus on the greater good. I am afraid I have to let it be." Ebony rolls her eyes and laughs.

"I am wondering about Danika and this guy. I hope she is not getting involved with him. She is just too young." I begin to worry, yet feel a sense of relief that she may let go of her obsession over Nathanial.

"She will be fine. She's probably just making friends," Ebony reassures me. "Worrying so much isn't good for you or all the people you worry too much about. Plus you don't wanna get wrinkles." She jokes.

The bell rings, and we all start to head to our classes. I watch Danika say "Goodbye" and go to class as the boy she was with turns and walks out the door. I find this a little peculiar, but I will ask her later at home.

◆ ◆ ◆

After the wonderful blood meal Florence prepared, I ask Danika to join me in the music room. "I just wanted to check in with you, girl to girl. We have been in Wenham almost three months now. How have you been coping?" I ask, attempting to find out more about I saw today.

"Pretty good. I will admit it is tough at times. One kid cut his finger in biology when we were dissecting frogs. I felt my fangs coming out, so I covered my mouth and ran to the restroom as if I were sick," Danika explains with a sense of pride over how she handled the situation.

"Good cover. Are you making some friends? I noticed you with a boy today." I had alerted Alexander of my concerns and he agreed to listen in without alerting Danika.

"Oh, him? He is just a guy, nothing to worry about. He asked me to hang out with him. I told him I couldn't, end of story," she says, appearing a little uneasy with her vague explanation.

"I understand. Just know I am always here for you. I know I was hard on you at first, but I realize I was wrong, and hope we can be friends."

"Thanks. That would be great." Danika stands with excitement and gives me a hug.

Alexander keeps a tight hold on our thoughts and informs me that Danika was truthful and is excited about me accepting her. He adds that she is concerned about letting the family down and that she wasn't thinking details, but her thoughts did have something to do with the mystery guy. He found it awkward that he couldn't get a full read on her. I decide to let it go for now and try to keep some trust between Danika and myself. I will look for this guy later and try to reveal his intentions.

Chapter Eighteen
Danika's Distress

"You can't keep coming around. My sister Sophia saw us talking yesterday and started asking questions." I look over my shoulder nervously.

"I'm sorry for that. If you come with me, you will not need to keep all these secrets any longer. You can live the way our kind is meant to live," the short scruffy male says.

"I can't. They are all finally accepting me as one of their own. The Pierce family is great to me, and I don't wanna disappoint them."

"Come with me, and you won't ever disappoint any of us. You won't believe the rush you will get with your first live feed, Danika. The fresh stuff is the best," he continues to pressure.

I start to think of what it would be like just to give in to my natural instincts for once. The glands in my mouth begin to water at the thought of a fresh feed, or "a hit," as he sometimes refers to it. I wonder what it must be like living underground like his clan does. My biggest question though is, "How are you able to be out in the daytime?"

"Although you are young, I am sure you know about the many powers in the world. I have the power of a light walker. I still have to avoid direct sunlight, but these cloudy days make it somewhat safe for me to walk about somewhat freely."

The bell rings to signal the start of class.

"I have to go." I demand.

"Okay, but promise me you will come with me to the club one night. You will not be disappointed," the young man insists.

"Fine, but don't come here anymore," I warn him.

♦ ♦ ♦

As I enter the school through the main doors, I cannot get the man's offer out of my head. *What was his name again? I can't believe I have forgotten. I am so bad with names, Drake, his name is Drake. I gotta remember that. I need to think of something else before Alexander decides to check in on me.* I have to wonder if things are as wonderful as my mystery man, Drake describes. The Pierce family has been good to me, but this is no different than my mortal life. I was attacked, Embraced, and turned into a bloodthirsty monster, and they will not even allow me to fulfill my needs. They have provided well for me, but I find myself wondering how others like us live.

Entering the class, I greet a few friends I have made and try to push these thoughts out of my head. We all make a little small talk before the teacher enters. One of the boys I have befriended, Jack, even asks me to the winter formal. He is a nice guy, not to mention very cute. But I think maybe I will check out this so-called underground vampire club after the formal. As the class settles, we all pull out our books, ready for a new day of learning.

Chapter Nineteen
Girls' Day Out

It's been a few days since Nathanial asked me to the winter formal, and me, Ebony, Matilda, and Danika, will go shopping for dresses. Constance will join us later. The boys decide tonight is a good night to play pool. I know Alexander will be analyzing Nathanial's mind, just to ensure he has proper intentions. Alexander is extremely protective of me, just as a brother should be.

My new relationship is actually quite frightening for everyone involved. Anyone and everyone can get hurt if my relationship with Nathanial goes bad. We all watched a relationship with a mortal destroy everything Caspian had worked for. I can only hope to learn from his mistakes. There is also the fact that I have never fully lived off human blood as he had for centuries. I try not to think about the repercussions that our relationship may have and try to believe in myself as we girls head to the mall and to hunt for the perfect dress. We search for hours, trying on all kinds of dresses.

Ebony picks a beautiful red dress and heads to the fitting room. "What do you think about this one?" she asks.

"It is perfect. The red looks so nice against your dark skin, and the cut frames your body perfectly," Matilda replies, showing off her keen fashion sense.

"What about this one for me?" Matilda asks, as if she did not know already.

"You are beautiful as always." I confirm.

Both Ebony and Matilda have found dresses, but Danika and I are still empty handed. It is hard since I am not into fashion the way Matilda is, or the way most girls are, for the matter. I enjoy looking nice, but in a more practical sense. I mean, what would I do with a Dior haute couture dress? I've always wondered who really wears that stuff. I threw out my corsets years ago.

Danika walks out of the fitting room, much to my surprise. I had not even noticed her going in there. "I think I may have found a dress," she says with complete excitement.

"Oh my, Danika! It's...it's just magnificent!" I can't take my eyes off her because she looks so grown up, a beautiful young lady. I have always liked her cute reverse bob hairstyle, longer in the front than the back. She is a very attractive girl, but right now she is beautiful. Everyone in the store stops to admire her in a gorgeous white gown, fit for a snow princess.

"The white of the dress on your fair skin makes your red hair blaze like the fire of the sun above. You are the prettiest thing I have ever seen," the saleswoman dotes in complete honesty, in spite of the commission she'll make on the sale.

"Thank you. I think we will take this dress as well," Matilda interjects.

Now I am the only one without the perfect dress and the formal is coming up quickly. Then it hits me, and I remember the most beautiful dress I've ever seen. It belongs to Constance, left over from her party days at Studio 54 in the 1970's. I guess we could consider it vintage now. I start to daydream about the amazing emerald-green halter-style dress, knee length in the front and floor length in the back. It has a V-neck bodice lined with silver accents. She also has the perfect pair of silver Dolce and Gabbana stilettos to match. The extra height will help since Nathanial is so much taller than I am. I start to get a little excited at the thought of having the perfect dress. Thankfully, Constance and I are both petite, she's about five-six and 110 pounds, I am only a few inches shorter, so we often raid each other's closets. Matilda is different, as she is almost six feet tall with the slender body of a super model. She actually looks like a young Grace Kelly.

As soon as Constance arrives, I ask her about the green dress, and she is excited about the idea. "That dress deserves a night out!" she says, gladly willing to let me borrow it.

After that's all settled, we head to the health food store. Ebony needs some herbs for her spells and potions, and the easiest way to get them without going into the city Wicca or pagan store is to buy herbal remedies and teas.

"So what are we looking for?" I ask.

"I just want to try out some truth, memory, and luck spells. I need to get some angelic root, hawthorn berries, and snake root. I also need to buy some candles–red, white, black, and green," Ebony explains.

Chapter Twenty
Hanging Out

"Well, now that we are finished with everything we had planned, why don't we meet the boys down at the local pool hall?" I suggest.

Everyone agrees, and when we arrive, they are all there: Elijah, Isaac, Alexander, Nathanial, and Matt. Ebony had told us that Matt had moved to Wenham in the spring of sophomore year and was the new kid until we came along. He is a really nice guy. He fought for her when she attempted to shut people out of her life after finding out she was a witch. She needed to figure things out for herself, but he adores her and waited for her to be ready to open up again. I remember he was the one who took her home the day she used her powers at school to put that nasty Mel in her place. Ebony has great timing, too, for she is finally coming out of her shell and letting him back in–just in time for formal. Matt has never given up on her. He even hangs out with us at lunch to prove to Ebony he will always be there for her. Just like I gave up pushing Nathanial away, she is doing the same. Last week, when Matt asked her to the formal, she agreed to go with him. They were friends before they became a couple, but Matt told Alexander and Nathanial one day that he has always felt a connection to

Ebony. Matt is different, and Alexander cannot read him, as if there is some kind of road block to his brain.

Matilda, on the other hand, sees much about him, as if his soul is an open book, pure and genuine. She calls him a "white soul," as pure as they come. Matilda has only ever seen one white soul once before. I remember the story like it was yesterday. Our family moved back to Europe during the 1950's. We met a young man by the name of Walter, a worker at the local orphanage.

"I was just thinking about Matt and how Mati told us he is a white soul. Do you remember Walter?" I ask.

"Oh yeah. Who could ever forget Walter?" Matilda says.

"Who is Walter?" Ebony inquires.

Matilda smiles at the memory. "We met Walter back in Europe. He had a similar soul to Matt's."

"What is his story?" Danika asks with sincere interest.

"Walter was one of the most caring men our family has ever met. He ran the local orphanage, where he, himself had grown up. Once he was old enough, he decided to give back to the only place he knew as home. He cared for each and every one of the kids that lived in that orphanage. Walter made it his life's work to help as many of those orphans find homes as humanly possible. Our family became benefactors to the orphanage after Isaac and Constance met Walter in the hospital one night. He stayed with a sick orphan all night long, holding the young boy's hand as he died," I explained.

"It was because of Walter and this young boy that Isaac became a hematologist." Constance says as she looks to see if anyone is interested in the story and then continues when she sees that they are. "Back in the 1950's, cholera was a major problem. The boy Walter brought into the hospital had a rare homological form of the disease, and we were unable to save him. His death took a toll on Isaac. After that, we became benefactors to the orphanage. That is when Mati met the young Walter and realized his soul was white, just like Matt's."

"That is a sad but interesting story," Ebony states.

Constance smiles at the thought. "After that, Isaac decided to learn more about blood. He never wants to be put in another situation like that again."

"Walter and Matt are the only two white souls I have ever met. The weird thing is, I still don't know what causes a white soul or what it means. Maybe one day I will figure it out," Matilda admits.

◆ ◆ ◆

We arrive at the pool hall through the window we could see the boys; they are horsing around as boys always do. I can see the smile on Elijah's face, beaming like a spotlight from outside. He enjoys normal human interaction and is happy we have made some connections in Wenham. This is the first time in a long time when we have actually been able to put down some roots and live with some semblance of peace and happiness.

When we enter the pool hall, Nathanial's back is to the door, and he does not notice us come in. I admire him. I can see just by his interaction with others and with my family what a wonderful man he truly is. As I get closer, I begin to take in the wonderful aroma coming from him. I stand and watch as he takes his shot and runs his fingers through his truffle-brown hair.

I sneak up behind Nathanial and wrap my arms around him from behind, running my hands from his waist up his rippled abdomen to rest on his amazing pectorals. Lifting myself up on my tiptoes, and I gently blow in his ear.

He slowly spins around and wraps his arms around me as well. "Hello, beautiful. Did you find a dress?"

"I have something that will do." I grimace, and he gives me a soft kiss on my cheek.

"Now that my good luck charm is here, I just might win a game," he says, hopeful.

"Well, I am here, but I am not too sure you could call me a good luck charm," I reply with a chuckle.

He just smiles and gives me a big squeeze. "You have got to stop being so hard on yourself. You are a wonderful human being, and I just wish you would realize that."

He is so sweet and convincing, to the point that I almost believe him myself. I smile back at him, knowing that no matter how convincing he is, it is not true. I can't be a wonderful human being because I'm not even human anymore.

It is now December, and it's getting colder outside, but the pool hall has a nice stone fireplace. Although the cold does not affect us, we decide to curl up in front of the fire, and we all order some hot drinks. Once the boys finish their game, (which Nathanial won), they come over and join us. Only those who are close to us know that Alexander and Matilda are a couple. Since we are hidden in a corner booth by the fire, Alexander slides beside Matilda, wraps his arm over her shoulder, and gives her a little kiss on the cheek– nothing too obvious, in case someone sees. That way, it still looks like they are nothing more than siblings.

I look at my watch and realize it is about nine o'clock, time to head home. After all, we still have two more days of classes before the winter formal. "How about I walk you home, Nate?" I ask.

"Is it not customary for the man to walk the lady home?" he jokes back.

"Nathanial, you live about two blocks away from the pool hall, and my house is a few miles away, just on the outskirts of town. Don't you think this makes more sense?"

He nods in agreement.

◆ ◆ ◆

We take off slowly down the dimly lit street toward the McCord house. Hand in hand, we begin chatting, always trying to learn more about each other.

Tonight it is his turn to ask questions. "Favorite color and song?" he blurts out.

"Red and I like a variety of songs. I could list a favorite from any decade really. I like anything Frank Sinatra, 'Alberta Bound' by Paul Brandt, most classical music and even stuff like Pink. I find classical very calming. I have always hoped to have it played at my wedding...maybe a beautiful waltz or something like that." I stop, realizing I am revealing too much.

"I will have to listen to it so I can learn to dance to it. Do you give lessons? I would not want to embarrass you." He gives me a little nudge and smiles.

At this moment, even though I think he is joking, we have an amazing connection, and I can tell he feels it too. It could be a possibility. I have all these feelings I never knew existed until he came into my life.

He continues with the questions. "Have you ever been in love before?"

"Ask me that one again later." I give a little smile.

"What is your biggest weakness?"

"You!"

"Me?" He looks a little concerned.

"Yeah. I can't seem to stay away from you, and I can't hide anything from you. Around you, I feel like an open book that has no cover," I admit.

"Hmm. Well, isn't that a good thing? Do you want to stay away from me and hide things? Is there some deep dark secret you are keeping from me, young lady?" he asks.

"Maybe just a few," I say in a joking manner, even though it's the truth. Even though I love being with him every minute that I can, I am glad we are finally at his house, because his questions are getting more dangerous than he knows.

We say our goodnights and our goodbyes, but as I turn to walk back to the pool hall, he pulls me back, spinning me around to face him. Then he gently kisses my forehead, then my nose, and then our lips meet, pressing ever so gently against one another.

"Goodnight, my sweet Sophia," he whispers, weakening my knees with his breath.

I turn again to leave, still holding Nathanial's hand. Our fingers start to slide through each other's until we are fingertip to fingertip.

"See you in my dreams." I wink.

He enters his house, and I take off as fast as I can.

♦ ♦ ♦

I am back at the pool hall in seconds. Matt has already taken Ebony home, so our family decides to go hunting for food. Isaac just got another fresh batch of donated blood from the hematology clinic. Because our house is near the outskirts of town, we are near the forest, which is perfect for our hunting trips. There is a vast array of animals to choose from, so we always catch something, but we are careful never to drain them to death.

"I have all the supplies to bank the animal blood in the trunk of my car. Do you ladies want to come or just go back to the house?" Isaac offers.

"I would like to come tonight. I am in the mood for a good chase," Florence says, and the rest of us agree.

After the hunt, tonight, like so many other nights, I dream of Nathanial and the life we could have had if we had only met a hundred years earlier. I dream of growing old with him, of having a family and children and grandchildren of our own. It is wonderful and perfect, but then reality sets in. Vampires only get the ever after–without the happily.

Chapter Twenty One
Dreams and Nightmares

Two days have flown by, and it's already time for the winter formal. Constance and Matilda help me get ready, because they love to dress me up like a Barbie doll.

Matilda curls my hair in loose ringlets. "Sophia, will you stop fidgeting? I don't want to burn you!" Matilda demands.

"Who cares? It's not like it would hurt!" I joke back.

With slight annoyance, she responds, "That's not the point."

Constance brings in the outfit I asked to borrow, along with an amazing tiffany headband. She volunteers to do my makeup for me.

"Thank you so much, Constance and Mati. I have the best sisters."

Suddenly, I hear a slight gasp, followed by Florence announcing, "Oh, Sophia! You are stunning, absolutely breathtakingly beautiful. I always knew it. You shouldn't try so hard to hide it."

"Thanks. I guess I'm trying to just be myself and not hide my true personality anymore," I defend myself.

"Don't forget your day crystal," Florence reminds.

Matilda grabs my necklace off the vanity and assists me in putting it on.

"I guess we are all ready. Shall we go?" I ask.

Alexander, Matilda, Danika, and I all jump in to Isaac's sports car, a beautiful black Jaguar with tinted windows. Alexander told Nathanial he will drive all of us, since Nathanial's house is on the way to the school. That way, Nate won't have to borrow his mother's car. We pull up in front of the McCord house, and Nathanial comes running out.

"What a sweet ride!" he announces, admiring the Jaguar.

"It is our uncle's," Alexander explains.

We all get out and head up the walk toward the house. Once Nathanial catches a glimpse of me, he stands motionless, like a deer caught in headlights. If I could, I would blush in this very moment. He looks so handsome in his tuxedo; once again, I am stunned by his perfection.

Nathanial finally catches his breath and stutters, "I have never seen such a beautiful sight in all my life. You are much more beautiful than all the stars in the heavens."

I gasp, wondering how he can think so highly of me. I am nothing more than a murderous animal that could easily take away everything as he knows it. "Thank you. You look amazing too," I say and run into his arms.

"Come meet my parents. I have told them all about you," he encourages.

As we approach the door, Nathanial's parents greet us. "Please come in from the cold, kids."

We all smile at each other before entering, and Alexander telepathically adds, "Thank God they asked us in. I hate that we have to be invited before we can enter another's dwelling, and it's always hard to make excuses for it. I'm glad Nathanial and his family are so polite."

The McCord home is very modest, but warm and inviting. I feel so much love within these walls.

"Hello, Mr. and Mrs. McCord. My name is Sophia, and this is my brother Alexander and my sisters Mati and Danika. It's nice to meet you." I am glad Danika's date just lives a few houses down, so he will be meeting her here to escort her to formal.

"The pleasure is all ours. We have heard so much about all of you, and it is nice to meet teenagers with such wonderful manners," Mrs. McCord replies. "Nate speaks very highly of you, Sophia. It is nice to see him so passionate about something other than football and school," she adds.

"Mother, do you mind?" Nathanial blushes.

"Sorry, love. You kids have fun tonight and be safe. Please call if you need a ride home or anything," she offers.

"Thank you. That is very kind of you, ma'am," Alexander replies.

After a few pictures, we say our goodbyes and head back to the car. Danika's date is waiting for her on the front walk. She introduces everyone and hops in her date's car to head to the formal. Nathanial opens the car door and helps me into the back seat. Alexander follows suit and assists Matilda into her seat, then gracefully shuts the door. The two of them walk around to the other side of the car and hop in. Alexander drives cautiously to the school, so as not to alarm Nathanial with his usual speed-demon driving skills.

♦ ♦ ♦

Once we arrive, I observe the beauty around us. We proceed to walk under a canopy of white lights that looks like stars. It is enchanting, and every couple pauses for a portrait lit by the hanging lights and the full moon that hangs perfectly in the horizon of the night sky. Nathanial and I pause for our portrait, followed by Alexander and Matilda, and then the four of us together. It is perfect. I know I will never get to see heaven, but this is what I imagine it would be like if I did.

Matt and Ebony arrive just after us, in Matt's '69 Shelby Cobra GT 500. It belonged to his grandfather, and Matt rebuilt it by himself, something he is extremely proud of. He did an amazing job, as if the car was rebuilt by Foose himself. He even thought of entering it in a car show, and now that I see it, I understand why and think he most definitely should.

We all enter the gymnasium under an archway wrapped in spruce branches and accented with white roses and red berries. Inside, thousands of little white lights twinkle, and lighted snowflakes hang from the ceiling. A disc jockey is playing a variety of music that almost everyone is dancing to. Throughout my years, I have seen many dances, formals, and proms, but nothing has ever compared to the perfection of this one. I wonder if it is because of the scenery or the company I am sharing the evening with. I now understand that love does brighten the world. Everything is better when you have love.

Nathanial guides me to the dance floor; it is like the parting of the red sea, as everyone moves to either side to make room for us. The music slows, and Nathanial extends his arm, offering me his hand. "May I have this dance?" he requests.

"You may." I smile as he places one hand on the small of my back and raises our joined hands up. I place my other hand on his broad shoulder.

Just when I am thinking this is a perfect first dance together, I realize what song is playing, and I look at him in amazement.

"I told you I would remember." He smiles.

"Thank you," I whisper. "I can't believe you got them to play good old Blue Eyes, Frank Sinatra, for me!"

"This is beautiful. I think I have even heard it before. But it is not nearly as beautiful as you are. I understand why you like it. Maybe it can be our song now?" he suggests.

"Hmm. That would be okay, but I heard another song that suits us much better," I reply.

"Really? And what song is that?"

I wink at Alexander, and he goes to request it.

Seconds later, Nickelback's "*Never Gonna Be Alone*" begins to play, and Nathanial smiles at me. "This is perfect. It describes exactly how I feel, especially if I were to lose you."

"I feel the exact same way. I could have written the song lyrics myself." I lean in and give him a small kiss, happy that we have found our perfect song. I can't stop myself from looking into his big ocean-blue eyes as the song ends and he embraces me in his arms so tightly. The music picks up again, and everyone begins bobbing to the beat and cheering. We decide to escape and go for a walk in the park to be alone. We can never get enough alone time. People still stare at us, shocked that Nathanial finally has a girlfriend.

I look over at Alexander to tell him our plan, and he nods in agreement. I know he will be listening in at least a little; he is very protective of me. It's like he doesn't think I can take care of myself, but I know he is really just concerned that I can't control myself. Sometimes I worry too. Nothing has ever appealed to me with such force and strength before. I refuse to give in to the temptation, no matter how hard I have to fight myself. I would rather leave him and know he is safe than to harm him with my love and desire. For that reason, though, I am grateful that Alexander will be close by. I want to taste Nathanial's blood. I crave it. But even more than that, I want to be with him. That is the main thing that keeps me from going on a complete and utter feeding frenzy. This man means everything to me, and over the course of just a few months, I have found everything I have ever wanted, and I found it in him. I do not mind the extra precautions, though, I'd rather be safe than sorry.

After losing Caspian everyone is secretly concerned about my relationship with Nathanial. They know he appeals to me even more than Caspian's girlfriend had to him. They feel my pain and torment when Alexander connects us all. I will make them understand. Nathanial is the only one for me, and now that I have accepted him as my soul mate, I am comfortable letting myself go, knowing that he will never let me fall. With Alexander close by, I feel even more confident with that fact.

Chapter Twenty Two
Saving

We sneak out of the dance and cross the street into the park. It is dark, lit only by the moon, which is shining like a big blue diamond, reflecting off the blue in Nathaniel's eyes as if they are a piece of each other. The park is quiet and very peaceful with only the faint booming of the bass coming from the school gymnasium. The sound mimics a beating heart and turns into a faint pulse the further we get. In an unusual way, the beating calms me and helps curb my urges.

From what I have learned, Wenham is a typical small town, a safe town, the kind of town where people leave their doors unlocked at night. Nathanial and I don't speak much. We just enjoy the starry sky and being in each other's company. Nathanial, being the gentlemen he is, offers me his jacket, but I am fine because the weather does not affect me. It is one of the perks of being immortal, I guess.

We get about halfway through the park when I suddenly freeze where I stand.

"What's wrong?" he questions with concern.

"I hear something," I whisper.

My eyes widen. I can't read minds like Alexander can, but I have a bad feeling, and I feel it heading straight toward us. In my head, I scream for Alexander, hoping he is spying on us and will be here soon. This feels bad–real bad.

Then, out from behind the bushes, a man appears. He is not from around here, and he is very rough around the edges. He has long, stringy hair, tattered old clothes, and he is very dirty. The man looks as though he had been traveling a while, and he seems tired and hungry.

"Stay where you are!" he orders.

"Keep behind me," Nathanial whispers as he braces his arm in front of me. "Can we help you?" Nathanial asks in a monotone voice.

Any member of my family could take this idiot down in a nano second, but that would draw unwanted attention to us and raise questions I am not quite ready to answer.

I begin to panic. *Should I protect Nathanial and deal with this moron, or should I wait for Alexander to come? I do not want to give away my secret, but I can't stand the fact that Nathanial is in immediate danger while I can protect him.*

That is when I hear Alexander, who is finally linked with my mind. "I am on my way. Be there in a second," he says.

I know everything will be okay. We can take this man down as a team, and Nathanial will not even realize what happened.

The man approaches us and presses a knife to Nathanial's abdomen. He demands our money and possessions.

Just then, Alexander runs up, startling the man, but suddenly Nathanial collapses to the ground. I can smell his blood spilling everywhere, it is intoxicating.

Before I even realize what is happening, the man jumps on Nathanial, and I notice a flash of red eyes and fangs glistening in the moonlight. He bites Nathanial's neck and tries to feed. Almost as fast, Alex rips the rogue vampire off of Nathanial.

"Sophia, are you okay? You have to take care of Nathanial. I will handle this scum." Alexander orders.

Matilda is already on the phone with our family. They will be here in a moment. This is about to become the biggest fight of my existence thus far–the fight to save the man I love, to save Nathanial.

Nathanial is lying helpless on the ground beneath me, bleeding to death from the knife wound and injured from the vampire bite. I start to worry about the venom and then realize it will not harm him as long as he doesn't ingest any vampire blood. When Alexander startled the attacker, he reflexively jabbed the knife in to Nathanial's abdominal cavity, twisting it and pulling it out in a downward motion before trying to feed on him.

"Everything will be okay, Nate. I will take care of you." I comfort him and try to hide my concern.

He begins to moan and grunt in pain. His blood continues to spread, and it fills my nostrils, smelling better than I ever imagined it could. I want his blood so badly, but NO! I want him more. I place my hands over his wound and began to visualize it repairing from the inside out. My throat begins to burn, and my jaw aches, I feel my teeth growing from the bone. I continue by visualizing a bright gold light around him, protecting him and healing him.

He opens his eyes and weakly smiles at me.

"You're...okay?" He can barely get the words out.

"I am and you will be too. I promise."

I do not want him to look in my eyes. They are not green anymore, but jet black because of the presence of his blood. His blood is affecting me, and it is so hard to resist I must fight it because I love him and never want to harm him. I can only hope Isaac gets here soon.

I look around to see what is happening with Alexander and the other vampire. They have gone deeper into the woods, but I can hear them and faintly see them. It looks as though Alexander needs help. A hungry vampire is strong and desperate. He tasted Nathanial and wants to finish feeding.

The rest of my family arrives just in time. Isaac runs off to help Alexander finish the job and destroy the vampire. It ends quickly, and they both return to the park.

"Sophia, that's enough. We need to keep a small wound to explain things. Work on the bite now." Isaac instructs me to finish the healing, as he takes over care.

Matilda pulls me off to the side to talk me down. A crowd is starting to form, and I am so thirsty. Constance is on the phone with 911 and Florence begins working on Nathanial's memories of the attack. He cannot have any recollection of me healing him and Alexander getting to us so fast–not to mention the vampire jumping him and feeding. I don't think he noticed Alexander fighting because they went into the forest pretty fast. I feel so weak, emotionally and physically, and the temptation of Nathanial's blood has taken everything out of me. What little energy I have left is draining from when I healed him. I am sick with worry, and panic is setting in again. I collapse to my knees, completely weak and helpless. I need to feed and to free my mind. I need to remain strong for my Nathanial.

The ambulance arrives at the same time as Elijah, who had gotten the McCords. He began to explain what he knew from Matilda's phone call.

Mrs. McCord runs to Nathanial's side. "Thank you for helping my baby," and she climbs into the ambulance with Nathanial, as does Isaac.

Constance and the rest of us will quickly go for something to eat before we go to the hospital. We have to eat before heading there, if for no other reason than to get the scent of Nathanial's blood out of our systems. Isaac and Constance want to be his doctors, since no one else will be able to make sense of his injuries and would have many questions. This way they can protect our secret.

Once we disappear into the woods, my family tries to calm me. Tonight we will hunt the old-fashioned way, feeding directly from the live animals we catch.

"Sophia, everything is alright. Nate is going to be fine. You did what you needed to do to help him, and you resisted the temptation. I am proud of you." Florence holds me in a motherly fashion. She has always been an amazing mother figure for us.

"It was so hard. I wanted his blood so bad. I wanted to change him so I could keep him forever. I just could not do that to him, to his family." I confess.

"It is all over now. Let's get you fed and go check on Nate. We can talk more later on, but right now, we need to be there for him," Constance says and holds my hand momentarily.

Chapter Twenty Three
Over Night

We're only about ten minutes behind the ambulance. When we arrive at the hospital, Nathanial's parents run up to me, concerned about the blood on my dress. "My dear, are you okay? Did you get hurt?" Mrs. McCord frantically checks me for injuries.

"I'm fine. Nate protected me and kept me from getting hurt. I'm just a little shaken up and worried. Is he...is Nate going to be okay?" I ask, panicking a little.

"Your uncle says he has no internal injuries. Everything is superficial and just needs a few stitches and a little bit of blood through his IV because the knife nicked an artery. It is a miracle he wasn't hurt worse than that. Your uncle said you helped Nate by putting pressure on the wound," she reassures me. "Thank you for saving our baby." she adds as she sheds a few tears.

"Miss, may I ask you a few questions?" requests a tall man in a police uniform. "My name is Officer Smith, and I'm here to investigate the attack," he adds.

"Yes, of course. Anything you need, Officer," I reply as I look to Elijah.

I follow the officer into a small room dedicated to interviews. Elijah follows, being that I am technically a minor and cannot be questioned without a guardian or lawyer present, and he is both. Elijah will observe as I recall the events of this evening for the officer, minus a few minor details.

"Okay, Miss Pierce. Can you explain to me what happened this evening?" Officer Smith pulls out a chair for me to sit in and walks to the other side of the table.

"We left the formal to go for a walk in the park, a man about fortyish, kind of scruffy looking, approached us from out of the bushes. He pressed the knife up to Nate, and Nate pushed me behind himself to protect me. Alexander and Mati had also come on the walk, but they were slightly behind us, and the man did not see them. When Alexander saw the man, he snuck around and came running from behind the man and grabbed him. This startled the man, so he stabbed Nate. The only thing I remember after that is Nate bleeding everywhere. I pressed my hands to his wound, like they teach us to in first aid class, until the ambulance came."

"Do you know what happened with your brother and the man?"

"All I remember is seeing the two of them struggling with each other a little. I didn't see a lot, because I was mostly focused on helping Nate."

"Thank you, Miss Pierce. Could you please ask your brother to come in?" requests the officer.

"Yes sir." I leave the room, and Elijah stays behind for Alexander's interview.

Out in the waiting room, I tell Alexander it is his turn, even though he already knows that since he was listening in while I was interviewed. He hugs me and then turns and heads to the interview room. He is prepared to give the same story as I did; only he will add the part I could not remember. He will explain that he fought with the perpetrator in self-defense. He will tell the officer that when he arrived, he placed the man in a headlock with one arm twisted behind his back. During the struggle, the man stabbed Nate, and the two of them fought. The man tried to stab Alexander but then ran off into the woods. What Alexander will not admit is the fact that the attacker was a vampire and that he and Isaac destroyed him.

Ebony and Matt arrive at the hospital. They run up to me and hold me as I collapse in their arms. "Are you okay? What can we do to help?" she asks.

"Ebony, I almost lost him tonight. I can't. I need him. I just found him." I sob.

"Sophia, Nate is awake, and he wants to see you." Mrs. McCord takes my hand and leads me to his room.

Entering his room, I see the most beautiful man I have ever laid eyes on, injured or not.

"There she is, my beautiful savior," Nathanial says in a raspy, weak voice.

I rush to his side. "Shh. Save your energy. I will stay with you...uh, as long as I have your permission, Mrs. McCord?"

"Yes, of course, my dear, as long as your parents are alright with it. I know he is in good hands with you. We will be back first thing in the morning." She winks.

The McCords hug and kiss their son goodnight. They say their goodbyes and hug me as they leave.

I can see that Isaac has various monitors and IVs hooked up to Nathanial. He needs to stay overnight for observation because of the blood transfusion, just to ensure a full recovery. He is extremely drowsy, drifting in and out of sleep, and I'm not leaving. I will stay by his side all night—forever if need be.

He opens his eyes for a moment. "Hey, sweetie. You are still here?"

"Where else would I possibly want to be?"

"I am so sorry." He reaches for my hand.

"What on Earth are you apologizing for?" I question.

"I'm sorry for putting you through all of this torment and anguish. I'm sorry for ruining the winter dance."

"You did not put me through anything. There was nothing you could have done. I am sorry you got hurt when Alexander came." I lower my head, ashamed at the memory of craving his blood.

"I am fine, thanks to you. Please don't worry that pretty little head of yours." He pauses for a moment and then continues, "I am just so glad nothing happened to you. If you had gotten hurt or worse, I just...I would not be able to live with myself," he said with pain in his voice.

"Really, you don't ever have to worry about me. Nothing is ever going to happen to me," I reassure him with more truth than he'd ever realize. I lean down and kiss him on the forehead and then wait for him to fall asleep again.

I sneak out to the waiting room so I can speak with my family. "What did the officer have to say?" I inquire.

"He didn't say, but he is putting out an APB matching the man's description, or at least that's what he was thinking of doing. Obviously they're never going to find him," Alexander confirms.

"So what happened? How did you destroy him?" I ask, wanting to make sure he will not return.

"When Isaac came, he grabbed a stick and staked the vampire in the heart. We decapitated him, and he self-combusted due to the stake. He is gone, no coming back. It was a difficult fight since he was so hungry. We will explain more later, but we think he could have been Cerberus."

"Oh that is not good. We will have to talk about it later. You guys should all go home. We don't need people getting suspicious. Isaac or Constance can stay with me and Nathanial," I suggest, and everyone agrees.

Constance decides to stay the night as well, and we head back to Nathanial's room. He has enough medication in him that he should sleep through the night. Isaac is transferring care of Nathanial to Constance. With that dealt with, we settle in to the large recliner chairs situated in Nathanial's room and begin a night of girl talk. I'm not sure if chairs like this are normally in the rooms, maybe Constance pulled some strings.

"Did you foresee what happened?" I question.

"Yes. I tried to call you but your phone was at home, so I called Alexander, but it was too late. It was after you left. I was putting things away in your room. That's why he and Mati were close behind you and why he was listening to your thoughts," she explains.

Constance usually needs to have some kind of connection to the person or situation in order to have a premonition. Touching my things must have given her the connection she needed.

"Is there anything else you should tell me? Anything I should know?"

"No, not yet at least, although I was surprised you chose to heal him instead of turning him. I know you love him," Constance admits.

I am extremely surprised with that comment, and she has caught me off my guard, but I figure there is no point in hiding it or trying to lie. "I do. I have since that first moment I met him, since I bumped into him on that first day on my way to class. As much as I want to be with him, I can't do that to him. It was extremely hard for me not to feed from him tonight. I have never been faced with such temptation before," I am ashamed to admit.

"Love is more powerful than anything else in the world, but..."

"But what?" I ask, wondering why she is hesitating.

"Well, I do see him joining out family in the future," Constance discloses.

I walk over to Nathanial, still sleeping peacefully. I lightly run my fingers through his truffle-brown hair. "I know we are soul mates, he is the other half of me. My life is finally complete, with him in it and Mati confirmed it, but I can't. Why would I want to damn him to a never-ending existence like ours? When I think about the reasons behind it, they are all selfish. I just can't turn the sweetest man I have ever known into a killer, a monster," I argue.

"I do not know the details behind his change. I only know I see him as a member of our family," Constance sighs and adds. "What is meant to be shall be, and we cannot always change it."

Constance and I talk all night and she assures me that Nathanial's pain is well managed and that his vital signs are good. It's funny, because every time I touch him, his monitors indicate that his heart rate increases a little; it is becoming a joke to us. When the nurses come in to check on him and speak with Constance, I pretend to be asleep. Constance takes a few moments to review hospital charts and records, make a few notes, and perform various hospital duties. Once the nurse leaves, we start talking again.

"Constance, I am just so torn! Nate is amazing. I could not ask for anything more from him. He has given me more than I could have ever hoped for, and because of him I have felt things I never expected. What on Earth am I supposed to do?" I plead.

"Enjoy him for as long as you can, but always know the option is there. Because he does not know any different, you can't possibly know what he might want," she reasons.

We agree to talk about some less stressful issues, and Constance starts to tell me how much she is enjoying her job at the hospital. "It is great here. Isaac and I fit right in, and the staff is very welcoming," she explains.

"The whole town really is great. I hope we can stay here for a while," I add.

I really believe the Wenham has a lot to offer us. The feeling of belonging I get from this town is really making me want to get to know the people better. If they can accept me, maybe I should try to accept them. I look over at Nathanial and begin to wonder if he will still accept me if he finds out what a monster I am. *How did Caspian do it? How did he keep such a secret from someone he loved?*

Constance and I reflect on the times when Caspian was around.

"It has been too long now, over thirty years. Maybe we should try to find him. Maybe we should bring Caspian home," I suggest.

"Isaac and I have thought the same thing. This might be something to talk to Elijah and Florence about."

It has been a long time since Constance and I spent the whole night talking, and it is nice to fully open up and express my feelings about Nathanial. They all know how I feel. It just feels good to open up and admit it to myself as well.

Morning comes quickly and my Nathanial awakes.

"Good morning, sunshine," I greet with a smile.

"Good morning, sweetie." He smiles back and says, "I could get used to waking up to you."

"Okay kids, I am still in the room!" Constance announces. She proceeds to give him a complete checkup. "One more day in here with the IV antibiotics, and then I can give you a prescription to take at home. Your stitches are looking good, and they can come out in a week. There should be no physical activity for six weeks, and do not lift anything over ten pounds," Constance orders.

"No football?" He looks devastated.

"I'm afraid your season ends here, Nate. I'm sorry." Constance hates giving people bad news.

Mr. and Mrs. McCord are back at nine o'clock sharp, and Mrs. McCord hugs me and thanks me again for taking care of him before she gives Nathanial a hug and kiss.

Nathanial repeats to his parents what Constance told him, and I fill in the parts he misses, ensuring they have all the instructions.

I say my goodbyes and excuse myself to go home and freshen up. "I will be back later."

Constance had me dressed in hospital scrubs so I did not have to stay in her soiled dress all night long, but I need a shower and some real clothes.

♦ ♦ ♦

At home, I clean myself up. I give Ebony a call to fill her in on everything that happened. I only saw her for a moment last night at the hospital. We speak for a short period of time and it is nice to have a friend to confide in. "How was your date with Matt?" I ask.

"It was nice...well, until we heard what happened. We were so concerned about you and Nate."

I assure her that we are both alright and there is no need to worry. "I will call you again later. Thanks for being there for me."

Chapter Twenty Four
Sighting

I decide to go downstairs and talk with my family about the events of last night.

"Sophia, I am glad you came down. Are you doing alright? You were amazing last night," Florence commends.

"I am alright. It was very difficult though," I admit.

"What you did, resisting your greatest temptation, proves how strong you are. There are not many who could do that, Sophia," Elijah praises.

I know what they are trying to say. I was able to resist him when temptation was the greatest, and that was a major milestone for me. I will most likely be able to resist feeding from him in the future. This is good, very good. It does not mean he is any less tempting, but now I have the true scent of him implanted in me and will not long for it as much.

"Well, Sophia, while you were away last night, we came to some revelations. I guess we should inform you of what we discovered," Florence says as she guides me to a chair.

"I hope everything is okay. What did you learn?" I ask nervously.

"Well, we believe the vampire that attacked Nate last night was a member of the Cerberus cult. We spent the night tracking disappearances and unsolved murders throughout the northeastern states," Elijah informs.

"What did you find? Have there been many?" I ask with concern.

"More than we would like. It appears as though they have risen from the wastes and are trying to live in the shadows. The problem is that they are hungry, ravenous for fresh, untainted blood," he continues.

Thinking of the bonds I have made here, I ask, "So what do we need to do now? If one has already made his way to Wenham, others may follow. I will not allow anything to attack this town."

"We agree, Sophia and will continue to work on it. For now, you worry about Nate," Isaac adds.

"So Danika, I have to ask, where were you when all this was happening? I don't remember seeing you," I begin to question. I can't stop wondering who that guy is that I saw her with.

"I was enjoying my first winter formal. I had no clue any of you had even left until all the commotion started. By the time I got outside, everything had cleared up. I looked for you and could not find anyone. I overheard someone say you and Nate got attacked," she defends.

"So that never clued in to you to check the hospital?" I become a little snarky.

"Seriously? Check the hospital for a vampire? Yeah, that was my first thought." She says rolling her eyes before she continued. "I asked my date to bring me home. I figured you would all be here and that maybe Nate was embracing."

"You thought I attacked Nate?" I scream as I jump up to get right in her face.

"No. I figured if he had been attacked, you would just embrace him. Try having a little more faith in me, Sophia-like I do in you." Danika storms upstairs to her room and slams the door. I can't tell if she is upset over my comment or the fact that I didn't Embrace Nathanial.

Everyone just stands in the living room in total shock. Danika and I have never seen eye to eye, but we have never had it out like this in front of the entire family before. I sit back in my seat and try to calm down a little. I try to trust her, but my gut tells me different. Maybe now is as good a time as any to bring up Caspian.

"So, Constance and I were talking about Caspian while we were at the hospital, and we agreed that maybe we should contact him." I slowly look around for my family's reaction. I know this is a sore topic, but I have to express my feelings about the situation. I want my brother back, for he is the only one who can truly understand my current torment.

"We understand how you feel, Sophia. We want him to come home, too, but it is his choice," Elijah insists.

"I mean no disrespect, but can we not offer a homecoming to him? Maybe he is afraid of what we think of him," I argue.

"I will agree with you there, and I will do everything I can to reach him," Elijah offers.

With that, I decide I will finish getting ready. Before heading back to my room, I pause and turn to my family. "Thank you for understanding. It means a lot to me." I hug Elijah and Florence and leave the room.

♦ ♦ ♦

When I walk through the door to my room, I fall on my bed and sob. Crying is not easy for a vampire to do, but the tears flow out of me so easily.

After a while, I collect myself, go to the washroom, and wash my face. I touch up my hair and makeup. I do not want anyone to know what I am really going through, so once I am presentable again, I begin to collect things to take back to the hospital for Nathanial.

I start to download some music and movies to my laptop for him, and there comes a knock at my door. "Come in!"

"Hey, Sophia. How are you holding up? I know this has been harder for you than you are letting the others know." Alexander closes the door behind him.

"I can't hide anything from you, so there is no point in trying." I wrap my arms around my twin.

"I actually wanted to talk to you about Caspian. I was surprised when you brought him up today." He sits on the end of my bed.

I sit next to him and ask, "Okay. Why do you want to talk to me about him?"

"I was just wondering if you remember seeing anything else last night." Alexander nervously twiddles his thumbs.

"No. Once Nate was stabbed and bitten, all my attention was on him. Why? Did you see something else?" I ask.

"Yeah I did. When I was fighting the rogue vampire in the woods, I think I saw...no, I'm positive I saw Caspian," he divulges.

"You know, I swear I have seen him watching us."

"Yeah, I know. That is why I wanted to talk to you. The problem is, I couldn't tell if he wanted to help me or the suspected Cerberus. I think we need to keep an eye out for him," Alexander warns.

"Alexander, I was closest to Caspian, and I promise you he would never side with a vampire cult, though I do agree we should watch for him."

"I don't want to tell the others yet, not until we are sure," he responds.

"Agreed. Let's talk more later on. I need to get back to Nate."

Chapter Twenty Five
Released

I believe enough time has passed, and it is now safe for me to return to the hospital. I stop at the convenience store to pick up some snacks for Nathanial and drag out a little more time, so as to not arrive back so soon. I finally get back to the hospital, and it seems like I have been gone all day. As I walk in the room, I notice some of Nathanial's friends from school are here.

Ben is there, and just like that day in photo shop, he insists on teasing us again. "Sophia, look at what you are doing to our man here. He is completely head over heels for you. Dude, what happened last night? Did you forget how to play defense?" Ben jokes.

"Hey, bro, shut your pie hole. You're embarrassing me." Nathanial says, glaring at him.

We visit with them for a little while, and then Nathanial and I spend the remainder of the day and night watching the movies I downloaded earlier. His parents allow me to spend the night again. I have to wonder why they trust me so much, especially since I know I could end it all in an instant. It is nice, although trying to push away from him was no longer an issue because we are becoming closer that I have ever wanted, and there is no turning back now.

I can't push him away anymore; instead I vow to protect not only him but his entire family. I will do anything for them. He is now the reason for my existence. I want the world for him, and I want him to experience everything I never could. This is my goal, regardless of what Constance said last night. I am determined to ensure that every single one of Nathanial's dreams come true.

"Sweetie, what is it? Are you okay?" Nathanial sounds concerned.

"Sorry. I'm fine. I was just daydreaming about you." I smile.

"I see. Well, I hope it is about our future, because I know you're in all of my dreams."

"It is about our future and all your goals. I want everything for you. My dream is to see all your dreams come true," I add.

"Sophia, all of my dreams include you now, so as long as I have you in my life, my dreams have already come true," Nathanial confesses.

For a guy everyone says, cares only about school and football, his priorities have sure changed. I don't ever want him to change his dreams because of me. He is so sweet and caring, and he has no idea about me. Here I am beginning to doubt my decision to be with Nathanial again. I can't turn back now. I love him too much. I will just have to keep him on the proper path and protect him in the process.

"I want nothing more than to have you in my life. I just don't want you to give anything up for me. We haven't known each other that long, and your feelings may change once we get to know one another better," I suggest.

"Sophia that will never happen. I have never been interested in any girl until that day you ran me down in the hall," he jokes. "But seriously, since the day we met, I haven't been able to get you out of my head, not even for a second. You are the most amazing girl I have ever met."

How can I argue with him? I understand exactly what he means, what he feels. I feel it as well. We're soul mates, meant to be together. The only problem is that he doesn't know why we have no future together.

With that thought, I decide to stop worrying so much and just enjoy spending time with Nathanial while I can. I crawl up on the hospital bed next to him and cuddle. While the movie is good, we talk the whole time. We enjoy leaning as much about one another as possible.

Nathanial likes to tell me about his older brother Luke, who will be coming home this weekend for Christmas vacation. "I really look up to Luke. He worked really hard to get into Harvard. I hope I can make my parents just as proud," Nathanial expresses.

"Nate, can't you see that you mean everything to your parents and that they are already proud of you? They just want you to be happy. You put way too much pressure on yourself. You are so lucky to have a family that loves you for who you are," I say with complete conviction.

"Sweetie, I'm sure your family feels the same about you. They want nothing more than for you to be happy. I just have not figured out why you fight it so much."

"I do, Nate, but I also know what it is like to not be appreciated and accepted. You are so blessed to have such an amazing family. I hope you realize what you have." I want him to understand, but I worry it is turning in to a lecture.

"I also know how lucky I am to have you," he responds and seals it with a kiss.

Lucky to have me? I wonder if he would still feel that way if he knew the truth.

♦ ♦ ♦

Nathanial gets discharged from the hospital today, Sunday morning. His parents are here and ready to take him home. I will go home and give his family some time together. I feel guilty for spending so much time with him. I am sure Mrs. McCord wanted to be with her son in his time of need. She was so gracious to allow me to be with him. As we are leaving and I say goodbye, I thank the McCords once again for allowing me to stay with Nate. I decide to offer my apologies for staying so much. His mother insists that she had to work anyway and was just happy to know he's been in good hands. That's a relief to me.

Luke is coming home from Harvard today. With his busy schedule he decided to live in the dorms on campus, coming home for Sunday dinners every chance he got. I thought it will be best if I stay away and allow his family to heal from the traumatic events of the weekend, so that's exactly what I do.

Chapter Twenty Six
Learning

My family had plans to go skiing today, but those plans change when Constance had a vision that we should stay home. She does not always share her visions, but we trust her to do what is in the best interests of the family. We learned early on not to question her or her motives. She always tells us what we need to know. It is best this way, and Constance has never done us wrong, so we trust her completely.

Instead of skiing, Ms. Edwina and the girls join us at our place today to work on their power control. We are the perfect candidates for them to practice on. Between the eleven of us, the skills and powers in the house are almost unfathomable.

"So what exactly are your powers?" Eliza asks.

"I can heal, Alexander is telepathic, Constance has premonitions, Matilda sees souls, and Florence controls memories. That is only the beginning. Isaac can control the elements, and Elijah can borrow powers of those around him," I respond.

"What about Danika?" questions Ebony.

"Funny you ask that, as we don't know yet. We're hoping we can find out with your help," Alexander suggests.

Eliza smiles. "So who has the strongest power?"

"Elijah's power is truly amazing. We try to keep it hidden, because this is a power many would love to possess. When one vampire kills another vampire, they acquire the power of the destroyed vampire, so it would be very dangerous for other vampires to learn of Elijah's power. They would want to destroy him for it. He is remarkable, and he only absorbs power when doing so is necessary." Florence beams with pride for her mate.

Now that we have disclosed our powers, we begin to discuss the powers of the witches. Ms. Edwina senses truth and lies, she has even acquired new powers of the years, but this is something we already knew. Ebony is telekinetic, so she can move things with her mind, as we saw at school. That leaves Eliza, and we have not yet seen what she can do.

"You must be wondering what I can do," she says. "I know you have witnessed both Grams' and Ebony's powers." Eliza raises her right hand.

We all look around to see what it is she can do, but we can't figure it out. Then, one by one, we notice all three of our witch friends are in different places than they were when she first raised her hand.

"You can move people?" I assume.

"No. Rather, she can control time. She can freeze time, and once she learns to control it a little better, she will be able to slow time and travel through it as well," Ms. Edwina explains.

"Why is it you were all in different places?" Danika inquires.

"Because her power does not affect Salem witches," Ebony answers.

As we learn about each other's powers, we also learn the major differences in our powers. Witches like Ebony and her sisters can learn new powers, and all the powers of their ancestors are somewhere within them. Vampires can only acquire new powers from the destruction of another vampire, except for what we bring in from our human lives, if anything–that is, with the exception of normal vampire powers such as super strength, speed, increased senses, and so on.

Elijah tries to explain a little more to our witch friends. "Because of the lifestyle my family and I have chosen, we rarely destroy another vampire unless they directly threaten us, like the other night. During the last Cerberus war, we fought, but we left the final destruction to others. We believe in the fight, but we have made a vow not to kill anyone, including the immortal. If we absolutely need to destroy a vampire, we will, when cases like protecting our own or those we are close to warrant such actions in our minds. In all our years, it rarely comes to that, and we are grateful."

"Will Isaac or Alexander receive any powers for the one they destroyed the other night?" Ebony asks.

"Actually, it appears as though he did not have any extra powers to gain. Not all vampires have extra powers. The Cerberus cult creates just for gaining numbers, whereas most vampires that follow Renata law only create if they can improve the clan with the addition of one and their power," Isaac explains.

"Renata law and Cerberus cult? Wow. There is a lot more to vampire history than I ever thought," Eliza admits.

"Yes. It is quite complex, and we will explain more as time goes on, but for now, let's work on your powers." Elijah diverts attention, and we all get to work.

Elijah starts working with us to teach us power protection, how to protect our powers so others like him cannot use our powers. He also explains the great emotional sense he received when around Nathanial. He believes Nathanial has a gift to extract emotional information from others, but because Nathanial is mortal, he does not understand this or how to use it. It just makes him easy to talk to, and that is why I have such a hard time keeping things from him.

♦ ♦ ♦

Everyone is having fun. Eliza's having fun surprising most of us, although she is getting frustrated that she cannot surprise Alexander and Constance. Ebony is doing really well too; she has been practicing moving items away from those who possess them. This may come in handy for extracting weapons from others. We continue working hard like this for a few days, and I lose track of time.

Out of nowhere, the phone rings. Constance and Alexander both turn and look at me, a telltale sign that the phone is for me.

"Good afternoon. This is the Pierce residence," I answer.

"Sophia, I have missed having you around the past few days. I think the doctor has called for my daily dose of beautiful," Nathanial says excitedly.

"I missed seeing you too. I just didn't want to intrude, with Luke coming home and you just getting home from the hospital a few days ago," I explain.

"Sweetie, Luke can't wait to meet the girl I won't stop talking about," he confesses.

"So would I. I could pick her up on my way over," I joke.

"Don't you be coy. You know you're the only girl for me."

"How are you feeling? Better, I hope."

"Yes, much, thank you. I get my stitches out in just a few days. That will be nice because they are feeling very tight and itching." He grumbles a little and asks, "So are you coming over?"

"If it is okay with your family, I could be there shortly," I offer.

"Of course it is. They are so excited that I finally found a girl I am interested in. I think they were starting to wonder if I'm gay." He chuckles.

"Sorry, but I refuse to share you with anyone, guy or girl."

"No worries there. You are the only person for me. See you soon. Drive safe, though, because the roads are getting slick," he cautions.

"I always do," I reply, leaving out that with my reflexes, nothing could ever happen.

The only person for him? But I am not a person–at least not anymore. I am a Vampire a monster. But I do know what he means and cannot analyze his comment as I always do. I really hate how analytical I am after so many years. You think I would learn let the chips fall where they may, but when it comes to this, I can't. He believes I am human, and I want him to continue believing it. I just know I will lose him if he finds out the truth.

Charlotte Blackwell

Chapter Twenty Seven
Predicament

The roads are pretty icy, but they are no match for my quick reflexes. I make it to Nathanial's house in less than twenty minutes. I made myself presentable before leaving and took my time not to raise any questions regarding how fast I've arrived. It has been a few days since Nathanial got home from the hospital. I miss him and can't stop thinking about him, but I kept busy. I'm excited to see him and don't even have the chance to ring the doorbell, before he comes flying out the door to greet me. He gives me a big hug and then leans down to kiss me. One small peck, and then his soft lips began to move passionately with mine. It is amazing how every time we kiss, it sends electric shocks through my entire body.

I hear a man clear his throat near the doorway.

"Sorry to interrupt, little brother." Luke taps Nathanial's shoulder.

"Oh, sorry, man. Allow me to introduce you to the most beautiful woman in the world. This is Sophia. Sophia, this is my big brother Luke." Nathanial introduces us while holding his arm around the small of my back.

"It is nice to finally meet you." Luke greets me by extending his right hand out to shake mine.

"And you as well." I shake his hand and smile.

He tries to pull me in to him and lift me to spin me around in excitement. For a short moment, I am surprised and resist, but then I realize what I am doing and release myself into his arms. I can see the puzzled looks on the brothers' faces.

"You're a tough one, aren't you? My God! You are freezing. Nate, let's get this poor girl in the house to warm up," Luke insists.

"Sophia, we have missed you. It is wonderful to see you again. Please make yourself at home." Mrs. McCord welcomes me with open arms.

"It is lovely to see you again. Thank you for having me over," I reply.

"You will join us for dinner, won't you?" With her striking wide eyes, she looks at me as she invites.

"Thank you. That would be nice."

I'm glad to have my day crystal so I can eat human food without getting those awful stomach cramps and indigestion, a normal and very painful reaction for a vampire. I begin to realize just how thirsty I am, because I have not eaten much since Friday after Nathanial's attack. I am going to have to watch myself and be very careful. I am sure Florence will have a nice blood meal ready when I return home. I got too caught up in training with the witches. I have only snacked a little. "May I help you with anything?" I offer, as Florence has always made sure we keep our manners.

"No thank you. Please enjoy your time with the boys. I think Nate has missed you a little and I'm sure Luke would like to get to know you," Mrs. McCord informs.

I am excited to get to know him as well. Luke means so much to Nathanial, and I cannot wait to get to know the man he idolizes so much. I am actually kinda nervous. I normally don't care much for what others think of me, but tonight I care more than I could ever expect to.

Nathanial holds my hand and leads me to the family room, with Luke in tow. "Are you feeling okay?" Nathanial asks with concern.

"I am fine. Why do you ask?"

"You just seem a little pale, and your eyes are darker. Are you getting sick?"

"Probably just a lack of sleep and too much shopping." I know that is not the real reason, but I cannot tell him the truth.

He gives me a little kiss on my cheek. "Promise me you will take care of yourself."

"I promise." I give him a little smile.

Luke begins telling us all about his classes at Harvard. "I am majoring in history." He starts explaining about the section on the Salem witch trials. He is particularly enjoying it because of how close to home it all happened. He decided to do a report on Sara Good, the woman from Wenham that was hanged in 1692 for being a witch and how she was wrongly convicted. We continue to discuss the topic for a while. Luke looks impressed by my knowledge of history.

"I did a little research when my family decided to move here," I explain.

"Did you know the civilians of Salem tried to persecute even more women in the late 1800's and early 1900's?" Luke adds.

"I read a little about that." I do not admit I was there.

He pulls out some of his textbooks. "You may enjoy this then." Luke offers the book to me.

Nathanial quickly grabs one of the texts for a closer look. "What the…?" Nathanial gasps.

"What's wrong?" Luke questions, and I await a response.

"This picture! The woman looks just like you!" He stares at the book in shock.

Luke takes the book for a better look. "Holy crap! She sure does."

When I look at the picture, I am shocked. It is me, along with my family. I try to cover my surprise. "Wow, it sort of does. That's so cool and a little creepy." I say casually, trying to brush it off.

"How is it possible? I know this picture was taken after the witch trials, but it is still from the nineteenth century. Do you have ancestors who lived in Salem?" Luke questions.

"Uh...um...well, I'm really not sure. I don't think so. The Pierce family adopted me years ago in Italy, which is where I was born," I try to explain.

"Adopted you and your twin brother Alexander?" Nathanial asks with surprise.

"Yeah, that's right. They came to Italy and found us, which is when Alexander and I became part of the Pierce family," I confirm stiffly. I start to panic, knowing everything can come crashing down any minute now.

"That's cool. Maybe I can help you find out about your birth relatives," Luke offers.

"I don't know. The Pierce family is the only one that matters to me now." I try to detour him. I never expected this. Who would have expected when we saved Constance all those years ago that the picture of us, claiming her body would end up in a history book. I can only hope I explained it well enough. I need to change the subject. Maybe I should ask Luke about basketball or about Nathanial as a child. I need something to distract everyone. I pretend to flip through the remainder of the book.

Just then, a scream comes from the kitchen. I can already smell the blood. Mrs. McCord cut herself, and Luke and Nathanial rush to her aide.

With my hand covering my mouth, I announce, "Sorry, but please excuse me. I can't handle the blood after everything that happened on Friday night."

I hurry outside to get some air. I feel the hunger taking over, burning inside of me, and I sense my eyes turning black. My head begins to spin and then pounds and I become dizzy. My throat and chest burn with hunger, and I know I need to calm myself. My jaw is aching, I can feel the teeth in my mouth enlarging and sharpening as my fangs start to protrude.

I look up and see Alexander there, ready to talk me down. I can still smell the blood. It is the only thing I can smell. I am sometimes grateful Alexander likes to spy on me so much. He is just what I need, and he calms my insecurities easily. He holds my head, forcing me to stare him straight in his eyes as he connects our minds and slowly calms me.

Luke and Nathanial finish bandaging their mother, and Nathanial comes out to check on me. Alexander hurries off into the bushes so he won't be seen. It is a close call, but because of his gift and our super hearing and speed, he is able to leave just as Nathanial reaches the door, assuring me he will stay close and connected.

As Nathanial steps outside, I glance up at him and become even calmer. He has such a powerful influence over me. I keep my head slightly lowered, as I do not want him to see my eyes, but through my peripheral vision I watch him walking over to me, his head slightly bent downwards, trying to see my face.

"Are you alright, sweetie?" Nathanial wraps a jacket over my shoulders and sits on the porch swing next to me.

"I am so sorry. I don't know what came over me." I refuse to look him in the face, for I do not want him to see my eyes. "I guess I am more upset over your attack than I let on," I try to explain. "You mean so much to me. I never want any harm to come to you," I continue, waiting for him to stop me.

"I understand. I was so worried that the man would hurt you, and I wanted to keep you safe, but I got hurt, and that hurt you. I want to protect you forever," he confesses.

"Nathanial, that is so sweet, but really I am okay. There is nothing to protect me from," I insist.

"Even if it is just protecting you from pain, I feel things for you that I have never felt before, and I never want to see you hurt or sad. If there is anything at all I can do to make things easier or happier for you, I will."

"I understand. I want to protect you as well, and that is something I have already failed at. You were hurt because I wanted to go for a walk."

"Our attack was not your fault. We should be grateful. If it was anyone else, they would probably be dead. Alexander is very protective of you, and his spying on us is what saved us."

I cannot disagree with him, because as he knows the story, that is all true. If any other student had gone out, they would probably be dead, killed by the rogue vampire. I may not have protected Nathanial, but some other poor soul was saved that night, and I can be grateful for that. Nathanial is only okay because of me and my family.

"Sophia, you have brought out feelings in me that I never thought existed. Some of the things you told my brother tonight were new to me. I never knew you were adopted or born in Italy. My point is, I want you to feel comfortable enough to tell me anything. I want to know everything about you, every inch of your being."

"I never think about being adopted or from Italy. I have been in North America for what seems like forever. It is just a part of the past and is not important to me any longer. I want to tell you everything, but some things are just so difficult to explain," I begin to confide a little.

"You can tell me anything. Nothing you say will ever change how I feel about you, and I will never leave you. I don't know if I could live without you now that I found you." He sighs and holds my hand gently. He lifts my chin with his finger to look into my eyes and continues. "I know we have so much more to learn about each other, and I want to know it all. I hope we can have a lifetime together to learn it, but why not start now?"

"I want to learn everything about you too." I smile ever so softly, slightly turning up the corners of my mouth.

"Sophia, I know it has only been fourteen weeks since we first met, but I knew from that first moment that you were the one." He takes a deep breath. "Sophia Pierce, I love you, and I always will. You have shown me what it means to live. Now I want you to share your life with me, and I want to share mine with you." He looks so incredibly nervous and, the way his hair is blowing in the light breeze pulls at my heart, he is so vulnerable and doesn't even know it.

Even though Matilda, Alexander, and Constance have all told me Nathanial and I belong together, this surprises me. I know how I feel, but I just never expected him to love me. I stand up, turn in front of him, and drop to my knees. He is completely still, not sure of what I am doing. I lean in toward him, resting my head on his chest over his heart. I listen to the rapid beating of it, a beautiful sound. All the hunger I felt has now left me and the only thing I feel now is love. "Nate..." I look up at him, running my fingers through his beautiful hair. "I am completely and utterly head-over-heels in love with you. I too, have loved you from the moment we met. You have shown me what love is and what it means to live with love. I have never met anyone like you, and I never thought I would. I did not believe I could ever deserve anyone like you, but now that I found you, I do not want to let you go."

He places his hands on either side of my face. "We were made for each other, sweetie." he says softly as he pulls me closer to him until our lips meet. They fit perfectly together, like two missing puzzle pieces.

Luke peaks his head out the door. "Hey there, lovebirds. Mom's okay, but we are going to go out for dinner instead."

Nathanial gets up and helps me up. He leads me inside. "Mom, Dad, I was wondering if the two of you would mind if Sophia and I just stay here? We can order some pizza and talk."

"Not at all, son. Just mind your manners and be the gentleman we raised you to be," Mr. McCord answers. He then helps his wife with her coat and prepares to leave.

"Mrs. McCord?" I squeak.

"Yes, dear?"

"I hope you are okay. I am extremely sorry about my reaction to your injury," I say, ashamed.

"No need to worry yourself. I am fine. Nothing a Band-aid couldn't fix. I understand. I hope you are doing okay, and please know we are always here for you if you need to talk...or anything. You and Nate have both been through a lot this past week, and I am sure it will take a while to heal emotionally. I just want you to know we understand what you have gone through and that we are here for you." The woman who–in any other life–might be my future mother-in-law hugs me before leaving for dinner.

Chapter Twenty Eight
Apprehension

As I gaze into Nathanial's eyes, I let the air escape slowly from my mouth. "Your family is amazing. They care so much for you and only want happiness for you, like they have found with one another. It amazes me how completely accepting they are of me, without really knowing me," I confess.

"I am very lucky. I do have a wonderful family, and now I have a wonderful girl as well. Nothing could ruin this. I have the perfect life." He grins from ear to ear, showing off his perfectly straight white teeth.

Nathanial grabs us some sodas from the fridge, along with the pizza delivery menu. We head to the family room and get comfortable on the sofa again. "I am glad we have some time alone. I think we have a lot to talk about now. I want to know everything about the woman I am in love with, and I have some questions I am hoping you will answer. I want to understand your past so I can better understand the present and future." He lays out his intentions in a sweet and calming voice.

Then Alexander interrupts my thoughts. "Sophia, be careful. He is suspicious. Florence's memory implantation did not fully take. The picture he saw of our family...he will not let this go. I think you should tell him, but tread lightly I will be just outside if you need me. He does seem extremely calm and content, so I believe it will be okay."

With Alexander's warning, I begin to freak out inside. Something I just hours ago I hoped to keep from him forever is about to be revealed. *How will he react? Will he be frightened by me? Repulsed? What am I going to do? How do I tell the man I love that I am a dangerous hunter that wanted to drink his blood, and that I am over a 130-years-old? Is he going to be disgusted by me?*

"Calm down, Sophia! It will be okay." Alexander's calming thoughts enter my head.

"Your family is truly wonderful. I hope you know how lucky you are to have a family that cares so much," I say, trying to avoid the inevitable and knowing full well I have said that before.

"I do. I just always worry that I cannot live up to their expectations. You also have a great family. They seem very caring, and I know I do not know them well, but Alexander is probably one of the best friends I have ever had," he confides in me.

"They are wonderful. My family is a great support system. They never judge and always help when one member makes a mistake instead of turning it into a lecture opportunity like so many other families do. Well with the exception of Danika, I tend to be a little hard on her."

I really want to ease into this, and I can tell Nathanial does not want to push me, though I can sense his growing anxiety and know that it will soon come out. I don't want to lose him, but that is what will happen as soon as he finds out that I am nothing more than a monster. My family has just got settled here, and now we're going to have to leave already.

Alexander speaks to me again. "Okay, seriously, sis. I told you it is going to be okay. You need to calm down, even just a little. Do you want me to come in and get you?"

Because our minds are linked, I respond back, "I can't help it. All I can think about is losing him and what happened to Caspian when he lost Ashley."

"That was different. She had no idea what he was, what any of us are, and she died because she didn't know the risks. It is better this way. Nate will be aware and can learn what to watch for."

Alexander is right, but I can't control my feelings. I have never been so terrified in all my years. I know it will be better if Nate knows the truth about me. It will be safer for him, and if he stays with me, at least he will be fully informed and it won't be under false pretenses. I try to mentally prepare myself, and it helps that Alexander is nearby.

Nathanial and I look over the takeout menu and ease into the conversation, both knowing it may be uncomfortable. He pulls a knitted afghan over us and just cuddles for a while as we chat. I know this can't last forever, so I try to prepare for whatever might come next.

Chapter Twenty Nine
Freedom

I think I am ready for this. It is time to tell Nathanial everything. I am ready for what he is about to ask.

"Okay, Sophia. I want you to know. I am in love with you, and nothing can change that! But I do know there are things you are hiding from me. I want complete honesty," he requests.

It takes every ounce of strength I have to not get up and run, but Nathanial calms me. He holds my hand and I instantly feel the peace he puts over me. "Yes, there are things I have been hiding from you, and for that I apologize. It is just that these are not only my secrets, but my family's secrets, and I have never shared them with anyone–at least not without my family." I take a deep breath, not knowing if I can continue.

Nathanial opens his brother's history book to the picture of me. "I know this is you somehow. I would know you anywhere, and I feel it. Plus, I recognize your entire family. I just do not understand how it is possible. Your family has not aged a day since this photograph was taken." He sighs and adds, "Since the attack, I have had two different memories. One is just like we told everyone, but when I dream about it, I see it differently. I see Alexander moving at unbelievable speeds and you healing me. My injuries were much worse than they are now. I remember feeling my body repairing itself, from the inside out. I have seen your eyes change color before. They go from the most beautiful green to jet black whenever you are around blood. You always seemed chilled, and you are pale most of the time. I have noticed your incredible strength, and you are so much more educated than anyone I know, especially in history. I know you are different, but I just do not understand how any of this is possible."

"Okay. I will explain everything. I only hope what I tell you will not change your feelings for me, because you mean the world to me. I also need you to promise that you will keep my family's secret, whether you decided to stay with me or not."

"I not only promise to keep your secret, but also that I will always love you, and nothing will ever change that," he tries to reassure me.

"This is not easy for me to explain. I really have never shared this with anyone before."

"I understand. Just take your time," he says peacefully.

So I take another deep breath and begin my explanation. *Here I go*, I tell myself and Alexander. "You are right. That is my family in the picture you saw. We saved Matilda from the persecution of witches in the late 1800's." I pause momentarily. "I was born in Italy in 1876. I was attacked in the streets one night by a vampire." I try to read his reaction, but I am more scared than I have ever been in my afterlife, and I can't tell what he is thinking, so I decide to continue. "Alexander was also out that night, headed to our family home. He found me and tried to save me, but the same vampire attacked him. Elijah, Florence, Isaac, and Constance found us. They were vampires that followed the six traditions. They decided to save us by giving us a few drops of their blood, and we began to make the transformation. They taught us how to live as vampires and to feed off animals and not cause harm to mortals when we feed from them. It is not as satisfying to drink only animal blood, but it keeps us strong enough. That is why we tried to safely supplement with human blood. We have all killed a human by drinking too much blood before, but it has been many years ago. My family has morals, and we find it more difficult to kill a human than most vampires. My family has found a new way to feed now, and that includes a mixture of animal and donated human blood." I sigh, "Well that is a quick basic explanation of my family." I notice the blood flush out of his cheeks, and his skin turns pale.

"Okay, so you and your family are vampires? Um, that is not quite what I expected to hear; honestly I'm not really sure what I expected. Are there other vampires out there?" he asks.

"Yes. They are all over the world, and not many choose to live the way we do. I also had another brother named Caspian, but things went bad for him, and he left, disappearing into the shadows," I explain, wondering what he will do with this information.

"I think I can be okay with it. I'm not afraid of you or your family. I know you won't hurt me, or at least I don't think you would hurt me...or should I be scared? I knew it was something. I just didn't know what," he admits with a hint of panic that he tries to conceal from me.

"No. You do not need to fear anyone in my family. You should just because of what we are, but we will never harm you, Nathanial. Quite the opposite, actually we want to protect you."

"So how is it you live normally? What about all that burning or sparkling in the sun or whatever?" he asks with a half laugh.

"Sparkling vampires? That's just for the movies. Burning is real, though, but my family has these things called day crystals–a magickal black diamond. A powerful witch placed a spell on them to help us live more like mortals. With the power of this crystal, we can eat human food, go out in the sun, look more mortal, and it helps us control our cravings." I show him my necklace. "As I mentioned, the necklace I wear is special. We all have some kind of jewelry with this special and rare gemstone in it. Matilda has a bracelet, Florence a broach, and Constance has earrings. Even the men have something. Alexander has a watch, Elijah a pair of cufflinks, and Isaac has a tie clip. Caspian had a ring that he gave back to us when he left. Once Danika was ready, Elijah lent her the ring. See, she is new to our family. Constance found her about eighteen months ago. We recently got her a day crystal of her own. There are others in the world that have the gem and those who don't have it want it. Without this little black gem, things would be a whole lot different for my family."

At this point, I am becoming concerned about his lack of reaction. He seems to be processing the information I just shared with him. He appears to be slightly concerned and maybe even a little disbelieving.

"Okay, so vampires are real, but so are witches?" he questions.

"Yes, and so much more, but I hope I can explain all that later. There is so much to learn, but I hope we have lots of time for explaining." I become wishful. "Please promise me, no matter what you decide about me from this point on, that you will not tell anyone–not even your family," I beg.

And then he leans over and kisses me. "Thank you for being so honest with me. I understand how hard it must have been for you."

I let out a sigh of relief. "How are you doing with all this? It is kinda a lot to take in."

"Strangely enough, I am okay. I want to know it all, and I want you in my life. I told you nothing will ever change my feelings for you, and I meant it," he reassures me.

I cannot believe it was that easy. *He just accepts me for who I am. I don't see one judgmental look coming from him—only love. How is it that even now, after he knows what I am, he still loves me? How can he love a killer? Nathanial is even more incredible than I ever imagined. How did I get so lucky?* Then I remember something that can end it all over again.

"There is one problem. Because my family does not age, we have to move around a lot. We can only stay in one place for a few years, a decade at most." I lower my head and add, "I want to keep you in my life and I just do not see how it is possible. Worst of all, you could get hurt. The only thing that kept me from feeding on you when you were bleeding in my arms was the fact that I love you so much." I lift my head and look at him with complete shame.

"It is okay, sweetie, I know you will not hurt me, and I trust you completely." He kisses my hand that he continues to hold tightly. "And you can trust me with your secret," he confirms. "Can you tell me about your other brother, Caspian was it? What went so wrong with him?" Nathanial asks.

"Well, that is a tough one to explain. Caspian has been gone for many years now. It is really hard for all of us, so we don't talk about it or him much. We lived in northern Canada at the time, and Caspian was a college student. He was eternally twenty-two years old, but he had been around since the seventeenth century. When Caspian met my family, he had grown tired of his ways, he wanted to find a new way to survive," I begin to explain. "My family agreed to take him in and teach him how to survive without causing harm to humans. He was doing great. He got a day crystal just like the rest of us and began going to school, and sometimes he would work like a normal member of society. Caspian wrote for the college paper and was enjoying his new life. Then he met Ashley, and they fell madly in love. She was mortal, and he kept our secret from her. Caspian found it very difficult, because he loved her so much, but he had a difficult time resisting her," I continued.

"Okay, so it's similar to us. The thing is, he did not confide in her like you just confided in me," Nathanial observes.

"Yes, and that is what concerns me. One night, Caspian and Ashley became intimate, and this is where problems arose. Caspian did not realize what his reaction would be. He had been intimate before, but always with another vampire who could handle his strength and not get injured. While they made love her heart started to pound harder and faster, and her scent became stronger. He could not handle it and became rough with her. He was biting, her tasting her blood, and in the end, he accidentally killed her." I bow my head, hoping I will never go through what Caspian did. "It was only recently my family share the entire story with me."

"What happened next?" Nathanial asks.

"Caspian could not deal with what he had done. He was so ashamed and could not face the family. He decided to leave. We have not seen him since. I sometimes think I see him keeping an eye on us, but he never approaches any of us." I sigh.

"I can tell you miss him." Nathanial pulls me closer.

"I do, but most of all, I am scared that I could do the same to you," I admit.

"Sophia, I am not concerned. You need to give yourself more credit. If you were going to harm me, the night of the attack would have been your chance. I was bleeding all over the place. You resisted my blood when it was spilling out all around you. I just wonder why you didn't just turn me. Then you would not have to worry. You can do that, right? Turn me in to a vampire?" he questions.

"I easily could have, but it would have been completely selfish. You have a great life and family that loves you. I would never want to take any of that away from you or your family. And yes, I did resist your blood that night, but it was not without temptation. My love for you just happened to win out over my hunger for your blood," I say with brutal honesty. *Am I trying to scare him away?*

"See. Right there you proved that you are stronger than Caspian was. You made the choice to save me rather than kill me, and for that I thank you. How could I not trust you? If you can resist while faced with such a temptation, you can do anything," he encourages.

"Nate, I just don't know if you fully understand. Your blood, your scent is so amazing. You appeal to me more than anything. Have you heard of pheromones? Cause that is kinda what is happening here, each person emits their own personal fragrance and as a vampire I am more sensitive to this. You are everything I want and need all wrapped up in a perfect body." *I guess part of me hopes he will reject me so that he will be safe forever.*

♦ ♦ ♦

Over the next few hours, we talk about my family and some of the things we have been through. We don't get through everything, as that will take a century. I do cover

177

the basics and answer any questions he has. He holds me with such love and admiration.

"How can you love someone like me? I have been damned. I have killed people before, and all the remorse I have can never change that. It is part of me. It is my nature to kill," I say.

"Because I love you more than life itself, and you can't choose who you love," he explains. "All the rest, we will figure out. We will be together forever," he insists.

It is extremely freeing to open up to Nathanial, and I feel so relaxed by it. He turns on the television. There is not much on tonight, so we just snuggle together. He eats the pizza we ordered, and for once, I do not feel obligated to eat for the sake of appearances. His family arrives home shortly after, greeting us and asking how our evening has been.

After all the formalities, I say my goodbyes.

"Will I see you tomorrow?" Nathanial asks with a grin.

"Would you like to come to my place? I know my family would love to see you again," I say. Nathanial looks for his mother's approval, and she nods her head.

"I would love to. What time?" he answers excitedly.

"How about I come pick you up around eleven o'clock?" I suggest.

"Perfect."

Nathanial wraps his arms around me in a loving embrace. I tuck my arms in around his waist. He lifts my head again and gently gives me a kiss goodnight. I can see his mom's approving smile. He then walks me to my car, opens my door, and leans down for one more little kiss. I watch as he walks back up to the house. He turns and waves before he closes the door. I fling my head back and let out a huge sigh. I do not deserve this man. He is too good for me. I relish in the fact that after so many years, I have now found something, someone worth living for.

Chapter Thirty
Distress

Alexander hops over the seat; he was hiding in the back. "That went very well." he cheers.

"Yeah, he handled it very well. I don't think it could have gone any better," I reply happily.

We both sit back to listen to the conversation going on inside the McCord house. I decide to drive away a little to stay out of sight. Our super hearing allows us to hone in on a conversation up to a mile away, more if we try and the conditions are right. We just want to make sure Nathanial was honest with me and will keep the secret. We are able to tune out the noise from the surrounding houses and zero in on the McCords. We can hear the family's approving words. Although they caution Nathanial to take things slowly, he has never been in love before. Nathanial admits he is indeed in love with me and tells them it was love at first sight. He also says he knows he wants to spend his life with me. In that moment, his parents seem to understand, as they to fell in love at first sight over twenty years ago and still remain happy today.

I can trust him with everything. He did not even hint to his family that anything is different. I realize that in his mind, the new information will not change anything. This makes me so happy, until I remember that we don't have forever. Nathanial is going to go to college, grow old, and die. I am never going to change, never going to grow old. How can we stay together?

"Let's go home, Alexander. I've heard enough." My heart is breaking because he loves me and I love him, but it will never work out. It is like a battle raging between my head and my heart.

◆ ◆ ◆

I drive faster than normal and when we arrive, the whole family is waiting.

"What is it, dear?" Florence asks.

"I can't do this. I just can't. I love him too much." I sigh.

"Can't do what? Was it too hard being there at his family's home? Did something happen?" Florence's concern is growing, and I can see the distress in her face. *Do they all think I did something?*

"No, nothing that hurt anyone or that was dangerous," I confirm.

"So what happened? What has got you so upset?" she asks in a motherly tone.

"Florence he told me he has two memories of the night he was attacked. When he dreams, he sees the real memory. Why didn't your implantation work fully?"

"I am not sure. Maybe it was because he was meant to know the truth," she defends.

"Sophia, it is meant to be. I can't give you all the details yet, but he will one day be a part of our family," Constance insists once again.

"No! I don't want this for him. Being around him is too dangerous not just for him but also for his entire family. His mother cut herself tonight, and since I have not fed in days, it took everything in me not to attack her. I had to leave the

182

house for a bit. I became extremely agitated and upset because I am thirsty. He knows everything now. He saw a picture of our family from when we saved Constance. I told him, and he does not care. He said he loves me and nothing can change that," I explain.

"Sophia, the two of you are soul mates. You and Nate belong together like no two souls I have ever seen before. You need to accept it, or both of you will be miserable," Matilda encourages.

"I just need some time to think, but most of all, I need to eat."

"I have dinner almost ready. Why don't you set the table for us, Danika? Everyone else can get cleaned up for dinner," Florence suggests. "You will feel much better after you have fed," she reassures.

After a delicious dinner, we all enjoy some lovely blood sherbet, and I admit I do feel better now. I explain that Nathanial is coming to the house tomorrow. I have a great family, and they are very concerned about me and are trying to make me feel better.

"Who is up for a race?" Isaac challenges.

We all jump up from the table and head for the door, already starting to run. Isaac always wins because he is the fastest, but Alexander is sneaky, reading our thoughts and ruining our technique. He is able to get ahead of Isaac and trip him up. The two of them fall to the ground and begin to wrestle a little. This gives the rest of us a chance to get ahead of them. We all stop at the same instant when we hear something beyond the trees: a couple of wolves. We are all surprised, as wolves have been extinct in the area for many years.

Alexander links us telepathically. "There is something different about these wolves. I think it is best if we return home," he informs us.

"You are right, Alexander. I see their souls differently than most animals," Matilda agrees.

"What do you mean you see their souls differently?" I question.

"Well, under most circumstances I don't see a soul on an animal; it is more like an aura. These wolves though are giving me much more of a human feel to them; I see the good in them. I can't explain it."

"It's the same for me, I normally don't hear animal thoughts, but I'm picking up some kind of gibberish from them. As if they are part human."

"I wonder if Ebony knows anything, we should mention it to her later and try to figure out what is up with these animals."

On that note, we all turn and leave the wolves in peace to return to our own dwelling.

◆ ◆ ◆

I am feeling much better. The fact is, I cannot continue on without Nathanial. I do not have the strength to stay away. I will just enjoy him and the love we share and go from there. What is meant to be will be, as long as he remains safe. I finally succumb to the full weight of my feelings. Nathanial means everything to me, and there is no hiding it. His family is just as amazing. I always wanted to be a part of something so normal and special. My family is great, but they are all I have, and after so many years, I think it may be time for more.

When I was mortal, the family I had expected too much from me. I was expected to save our family name and honor. It was too big a burden for such a young girl. Growing up back in Italy, I was raised knowing it was my responsibility to keep the family. I recall how my birth mother would explain my duties to me. I was expected to marry a wealthy and powerful man that would increase our royal stature. I was the firstborn daughter to the Suvanto family in over ten generations.

I remember back to the 1800's when I was alive, only a woman who married a royal improved the family's worth. Our family had been stuck at the same level forever. I was the one to improve that and bring more money to the family. I was to marry up the social ladder and reproduce for the royal family. Once I was married to someone of proper standing and I produced a male heir to become king, my family's standing in society would have been solidified. I sometimes feel as though the vampire that attacked me actually saved me because he led me to the Pierce family, my afterlife family. I am grateful to them for saving me from a tragic life. All I ever wanted was love, and finally, after over a century, I have found it, and I am not about to let it go. My mind is finally made up, and I will fight for Nathanial.

◆ ◆ ◆

My family and I thought now would be good time to tidy the house. It is nearly immaculate, but Florence insists we maintain a proper and presentable home at all times.

"Our home is the one true thing we have in our existence that we can be proud of. We never know when someone may stop by to say hello."

"Yes, Mother. We know," everyone grumbles at the same time.

While cleaning, we put the local radio station on, crank up the volume, and dance around our beautiful home. After so many years, we have a pretty good system and get it done in no time flat, even without using our super speed. We all enjoy the perks of being a vampire, if you can call them perks, but we enjoy being as normal as possible even more.

Our time together is enjoyable, and now that it is winter break, we have all kinds of plans to explore the area and learn even more about this little town we are beginning to call home. It has been a very interesting day, and the events have taken a toll on me.

"Where is Danika? I don't recall seeing her since we returned from the forest," I make known, thinking that like a normal teen, she is hiding in her room avoiding chores.

Isaac runs up to her room and back down again. "She is not there," he says with concern.

We do a quick search of the house, but she is nowhere to be found.

"My Lord! I hope she did not get caught up with those wolves. We better find her," Florence says with a slight hint of fear in her voice.

"You stay here, Florence, in case she returns. The rest of us will go look for her," Elijah suggests.

We all set out to look for Danika, running at top speed and tuning in to all the sounds we can find.

Chapter Thirty One
Caspian's Watchful Eye

December 22,

My formal family has been keeping me busy the past few days. I worry about Sophia, the girl I once called a sister. I can only hope her relationship with that boy–Nathanial–does not end like mine and Ashley's did. I almost blew my cover the night of his attack. If Isaac had not shown up when he did, I would have been forced to help Alexander defeat the rogue Cerberus. I continue to log my mission in my journal. It was difficult to stand back and watch Sophia and her mate get attacked by the Cerberus. I wanted to warn her that he was in the area and that there are more heading their way. I sense them.

My ability to sense others of supernatural force would be very helpful to my family in the coming weeks and months. Constance's gift of premonitions will help as well, but only if she has contact with something or someone involved. She has no control over what she sees. Another problem I have learned is that the leader of the Cerberus cult has the ability to block mental abilities of others. This is something he can use to his advantage, and he may have blocked all mental abilities in the area. There is no way of knowing.

When I left my family thirty years ago, I swore I would protect them and I have succeeded–at least until now. I am helpless when it comes to Sophia's dealings with this mortal, although she has always been emotionally stronger than I was back when I was with Ashley. I still worry about her. I need to trust that the family learned from my mistakes. I felt a slight moment of relief when I was watching Sophia tonight. Nathanial is now aware of what Sophia and the family is, and this alone protects all of them. I should have been honest with Ashley, but I cannot concern myself with that at the moment.

It is the new vampire Danika, I must worry about. She is trouble and quickly headed down the wrong path. I will do everything in my power to keep my former family safe, even if it means destroying their newest member. I have been watching the Cerberus approach her, attempting to draw her to them. It is difficult to watch, as I know her actions will affect the family I care about. I fight the urge to shake some sense into that young head of hers. I have no other choice but to join the cult undercover. I can't go back to my family, not after what I did, they deserve better than me and I still must atone for my mistakes. Leaving them was the greatest punishment I could ever receive. Now I must remain at a distance if I want to help them. They almost have her convinced to join them, to live as a vampire was created to live. I have watched as they taunt her with the feel of a fresh kill and the taste of blood as it pumps warm and juicy right out of its artery. They are after my family, and she is leading them directly to them. My family? I guess they always will be.

I need to be more careful. I have become sloppy and am sure a few members have seen me creeping around recently. They must not know I am here. I will go to the underground vampire club and offer myself. This will give me insider knowledge and keep me away from the family. Tomorrow I, Caspian Pierce, will become a member of the Cerberus cult in order to protect the ones that once protected me.

I finish my journal log for the night and place it in the safe in my hotel room. I have heard about Club VC before. There is one is Boston, and this is where I will find the

Cerberus. I remember when I made some vampire friends up north, they used to party there. I recall their explanations about Club VC and what I overheard from the cult members. VC is an underground vampire club, run by the Cerberus cult. I recall it being compared to Studio 54 from the early 1970's. Humans have been persuaded to work there. From my understanding, the cult searches for humans that are lost, runaways and the homeless, and then they use the power of compulsion to have them agree to become living blood banks. I will need to see the extent of this myself, so I try to find something funky to wear tonight. Locking up, I decide to take a quick pass through the woods by the house occupied by those I am trying to protect.

I watch from high in a tree as they all run by. In the distance, I can see two wolves. I thought they were extinct in the area, yet I get a supernatural feeling from them. That gives me one more thing for me to look into. The family stops and turns around to head back home. Some things never change, for Isaac is still in the lead. I notice Danika is a fair bit slower than the rest. As I watch her, the alarms within me begin to go off. I search the woods, sensing the Cerberus nearing. As I prepare to warn my family, I notice Danika winding off the path. I quietly follow her to where she meets the same vampire she has been talking to at school. I still need to figure out how is he able to survive in the sun, without a day crystal. Thanks to technology these days, I have equipment set up all over so I can watch my family during the day on my computer.

I watch the vampire pressure Danika: "You told us you would come and party with us after your formal."

"I know, but my sister's boyfriend was attacked that night by some cult member," she naively replies, not knowing he is a member of the cult and is all too aware of the attack.

"That is horrible. Why don't you come tonight?" he tempts in a snarky tone.

"I will soon, but my family has lots of holiday plans. Soon. I promise."

I make note of the sincerity of her voice.

I am realizing she really is not aware of whom she is getting involved with. I sense the family heading back to the area. They must have noticed her missing. The cult vampire takes off quickly.

"There you are, Danika. We have been worried about you. What happened?" Constance asks as she approaches.

"Sorry. I was just exploring the woods a little. I thought I was close enough to home that the wolves would not come near," she answers, trying to hide her plans.

"You can't be out here like this by yourself. You are not skilled enough if another vampire attacks, and we know they are around now," Elijah reasons.

"Sorry. I was not thinking. I will be more careful from now on."

The family heads back to the house, and I move on my way to Boston. I need to offer myself to the cult at the club. It is the best way to protect my family.

Chapter Thirty Two
Relief

"I am so glad you are alright, Danika. Don't you ever do that to us again, young lady!" Florence throws her arms around our youngest member.

"I'm so sorry, Mother Florence. I was not thinking straight," Danika says with remorse.

Walking toward Danika, I open up, "I know you are new to this family, but we care about our members very much. I am sorry for always being so hard on you. I am just taking my fears out on you. I'm sorry I was so mad at you tonight. I am going to try to let go of the anger and show you I care."

"Thank you, Sophia. That means so much coming from you. I will try to make you proud."

I notice her bite her lip at the end of that sentence. I have to wonder if that is earnestness or guilt. It doesn't matter, as long as she understands that the family was worried about her.

Everyone takes their turns informing Danika of how we feel about her and what our family means to each of us. She sits in front of each of us, and I can see her pain. She has only been a vampire for about a year and a half now, and in this time a new vampire goes through all the emotions of a person diagnosed with a terminal disease. Being that she is also a teenager, she is bound to act like one.

Florence brings in some blood tea infused with a little rum. "We had a little scare tonight, and I think a little relaxation is in order. Everyone needs to let go of these emotions we are having."

"Each and every one of us is so lucky to have you in our existence, Florence. Thank you for everything you do." Elijah leans in and kisses his wife.

We nod in agreement and enjoy our tea.

"I think it is time we turn in for a little rest," Florence encourages.

◆ ◆ ◆

I decide to go upstairs and clean up a bit. I take a shower and get into my most comfortable pajamas. I turn on my stereo and lie down on the bed, trying to relax and enjoy the music. It is classical tonight. I do not need much sleep, but tonight I am mentally exhausted. As I lie there in bed, I begin to picture the music, the notes dancing across the bars. It is beautiful to imagine the music coming alive like this. Music is an amazing thing, from the first note to the final melody. Until I met Nathanial, the arts were my one true passion. It has always been consistent and has always been there for me to turn to. I slowly relax and enter a deep meditative state, drifting off to sleep with the hope of seeing Nathanial in my dreams.

"Nathanial, NO! Please! I beg you...don't ever be like us. I want you to experience everything I never could," I plead.

"I want to be with you forever, Sophia, and this is the only way. I will find someone to turn me. We will be happy and will always have each other," he argues.

"I will leave before I ever let you be Embraced," I threaten.

"I will never let anything tear us apart, my love. I will love you forever and always. Even if you leave, I will find a way to

Embrace and walk the Earth searching for you. This is what I want and nothing more. How could I ever miss out on anything if I have you?"

"How can you do this to your family? To lose you would destroy your mother."

"My family would understand and support my choice."

I awake and sit up in bed, wondering if what I just dreamt could possibly happen. I do not want this for him. Being a vampire has it perks, but it is treacherous never growing or changing, cursed to walk the Earth forever. *He won't do it. Nathanial would never do that to his family.* I calm myself from the dream and drift back to sleep. As fast as I fall back asleep, the dream is forgotten.

Chapter Thirty Three
Welcoming

I go to pick up Nathanial at eleven o'clock, just as planned. He gets in the car giving me that wonderful grin I love so much. I'm nervous. It is just like the first time I met him, waiting for him to speak.

"I had some time to think about things last night."

My heart plunges into my gut as I wait for him to continue.

"And I want you to know that no matter what, I am still completely in love with you, I know it will all work out the way it is meant to be," he reassures me and leans in for a kiss. "Now I want you to teach me and show me everything," he says eagerly.

"Just remember...you asked for it." I say with an evil little grin. I hammer down on the accelerator of my Porsche Cayenne. "Buckle up, buttercup." I laugh.

We arrive at my house in no more than a minute or two.

"Holy crap! That was faster than Mario Andretti," he chokes out with a little shock in his voice.

I remind him that he asked for it. "Well, lesson one, I have superior reflexes and have been driving since cars were made." I smirk. "And you are right. That was faster than Mario Andretti. I could smoke his butt any day."

We get out of the car sharing a little giggle. Even though I am in the driver's seat, he still walks around to open my door for me.

"This is not a house. It's a freaking hotel." he gasps.

"It was actually a bed-and-breakfast years ago," I explain.

The acreage we live on is perfectly manicured, the drive is cleared of all snow, and the frosted trees glisten in the sun. The driveway circles around a fountain that is situated in the middle of a grassed area. Off to the right is a large attached garage that would make Jay Leno jealous. I park in front of the main steps that lead to the front door. We begin to walk up the marble stairs that lead to a beautiful wrap around veranda with marble roman pillars holding the roof above.

When we enter through the large French doors, my family is waiting to welcome Nathanial. Each member of the family lines the grand staircase at the back of the large front foyer. There are two sets of stairs, each in the shape of a semi-circle leading to the second floor. The décor has been collected throughout our years of travel, and the furniture has a contemporary feel.

"Your home is breathtaking. I could have never imagined anything so amazing," Nathanial compliments. "Thank you for welcoming me into your home."

"Nate, it is great to finally have you here." Alexander greets him with a handshake.

Matilda comes down next. "Looking good. I trust you are feeling better?"

"Much, thank you." He smiles.

"Nate, I would like to formally introduce you to my Aunt Constance and Uncle Isaac, the doctors that cared for you," I announce.

"We met playing pool before the winter formal," Nathanial reminds me.

"Oh, that's right. I can't believe I forgot I guess I have had so much on my mind."

"Nate, it is a pleasure to see you under better circumstances," Isaac says.

"Thank you for stitching me up. I just wish Sophia could have healed it completely. Now I am going to miss Christmas day scrimmage with my brother," he jokes.

"And last are my mother and father figures, Florence and Elijah. I guess you also met Elijah at the pool hall, but I don't believe you met Florence formally."

"Welcome, Nate. Our home is your home." Florence gives him a hug.

"You better take care of yourself. I don't think our girl could handle if anything else happened to you," Elijah says, shaking Nathanial's hand.

He smiles and says, "Thank you so much. It is an honor to spend the day with the family that brought Sophia to me. I am forever indebted to you."

"Well, why don't we go and relax in the family room? The girls have prepared some refreshments and baked some blueberry scones. They did very well, if I may say so myself," Elijah announces.

"Thank you. That sounds wonderful, but you really did not need to go to any trouble for me. I am just happy to be here," Nathanial replies with all the manners of an aristocrat.

"So, Nate, do you have any questions for us or any concerns we could help ease?" Elijah asks, breaking the ice.

"I do have lots of questions, but I know they will all be answered in time. I would really enjoy getting to know all of you and what your lives have been like as a family. You know the normal stuff, before we get to the other stuff."

"That would be lovely!" Florence agrees.

We sit and visit with my family for a while. We cover all the usual things like embarrassing stories from over the years, school, and Christmas, which is fast approaching.

"We should host a New Year's party. We could invite everyone and try to get to know the townspeople," Matilda suggests.

"What an excellent idea! We could invite the families from work and school," Constance agrees, always up for a good party.

"You better invite me." Nathanial jokes.

Everyone has a good chuckle, and he looks around.

"It wasn't that funny," he defends.

"Nate..." Elijah places a hand on his broad, thick shoulder. "The thing is our family takes love very seriously. Love is very important, and when you add soul mates to the mix. Well, what I am trying to say is that we already consider you part of our family. You are with Sophia and we all believe you to be soul mates. You never need an invitation around here. I hope that doesn't scare you away."

"Let me get this straight. You are worried that you just scared me by inviting me into your family? Let's recap the things that could have and should have scared me in the last few months." Nathanial begins his reflections on the past few months, and we all listen to the events as he sees them. "The first day of school, I literally bump in to the most amazing woman in the world. Falling head over heels in love. . I experiencing feelings I have never thought I would have. I know I can't live without her and everything I know is about to change. That was a little scary. Then, once I found the courage to ask her out, I get stabbed and have memories of unbelievable events surrounding the stabbing. That was a little more than scary." He takes a deep breath and continues. "Then there was finding out the love of my life and her entire family are actually a clan of vampires and that she wanted to drink my blood. I even found out that witches are real, yet not one of these things compares to the fear I felt when—"

"You came here?" Matilda interrupts.

"No. That was not scary at all." He smiles and looks over at me before continuing, "Telling Sophia I am in love with her and opening my soul to her was the scariest moment of my life because I was terrified she would reject me since we just started dating," he confesses. "So by comparison, being considered part of your family is a relief. My only hope is to make it official one day."

In shock, we all look at one another. *Does he really mean or even understand what he just said?*

"What? What could you possibly mean by that?" I frantically ask as the dream I had last night comes rushing back to me.

"Maybe we should save that conversation for a later date." He smiles.

I look at Alexander.

Nathanial says, "Let's keep this one between us, bro." Clearly, he has already figured out what Alexander's gift is, and Alexander only chuckles.

"Well, thank you for sharing with us. It was nice." Elijah smiles at Nathanial.

Chapter Thirty Four
Planning

"Enough serious talk. Let's get back to party planning. Constance and I can handle the decorating. Nate, can you assist Sophia with the invitations and guest list? Since you know almost everyone in town, you would be best at deciding who to invite," Matilda says excitedly.

"We can take care of the menu," Florence volunteers, and Elijah nods in agreement.

"Can I handle the swag?" Danika asks excitedly.

"Swag? What the heck is swag?" Isaac makes a goofy, confused look.

We girls all laugh, and Danika explains, "Swag is like a loot bag, a party favor bag filled with nice gifts."

Florence's smile reaches from ear to ear. "That is a wonderful idea, Danika. I would love to go shopping with you."

"Mother and daughter shopping spree. It's a date."

"I guess that leaves us with the entertainment." Alexander gives Isaac a nudge.

"Well, alright then. We all have our to-do lists, so we'd best get started. There is not much time." Matilda jumps up and runs to the other room with Constance in flow.

"So, Nathanial, shall I give you the tour?" I offer.

"Please do," he says eagerly.

Hand in hand, with our fingers intertwined, I begin to show him the rest of the house. Since we are in the family room, I decide to lead him to the library next, just off the family room and quite impressive.

Walking through the double doors of the library, we both look around at the room lined with mahogany shelving that slide on rails, revealing even more shelving. The ceiling is about twelve feet high. Every shelf is filled with books of every kind. A lovely hand-carved old wooden rung ladder is available to allow anyone to reach any book in the collection, even from the highest shelves.

"I have never seen anything like this before. It is magnificent." Nathanial starts gushing. "I know where I am coming to study from now on."

I laugh at his enthusiasm. "This is only the second room you've seen. Just wait!" I tease.

We move throughout the remaining rooms. The gourmet kitchen, the office, theatre room, game room, exercise room, and indoor pool. We continue on to visit all eight bedrooms, all ten baths, and the study.

"The art room is one of my favorites in the entire house," I admit as I show him the various instruments, painting, and other art supplies.

"Can you play any of these?"

"Yes. I can play all of them quite well." I grin. "But I prefer painting."

"Did you paint any of these?" Nathanial politely asks.

"Yeah, most of them."

"They are magnificent ," he gushes while examining the wall of art. "Why don't you play something for me while I look around?"

"Sure. What would you like me to play?"

"Whatever. I just want to see some of your talents," he replies.

I decide to strum a little tune on my guitar. I begin playing a song I have been working on since my family moved here. "This song expresses all the feelings I had in the beginning until now–hate, love, fear, remorse, and everything under the rainbow."

Near the end of my piece, it becomes very soothing and caring with a sense of acceptance.

"Wow! That was extremely moving. Who is it by?"

I can tell he feels all my emotion in the song. "I wrote it. It is a compilation of my feelings from our move to Wenham to meeting you," I admit.

"Well, I could feel how torn you were about us, but I may even understand a little better now." He leans over and gives me a hug and adds, "I am sorry I caused you such distress."

"It was not you that caused the distress and anguish. Being a vampire is what caused it. I did not think it was possible to love a mortal," I assure him.

We head back downstairs and to the garage, a place I know he will enjoy.

"This is my kind of garage." He begins to examine each and every car.

We have many different sports, luxury, and foreign cars, along with a few classics and average cars. It is any man's dream, and I knew he would love it here.

"I never knew homes such as this actually existed." He said flabbergasted.

"Let's go to my room and start the guest list," I suggest.

We head back up the grand staircase to my room. It is a large room, painted white with a large bay window and window seats that overlook the garden. I have a hand-carved oak king-sized bed draped with a bright red duvet. Across from the bed is a matching armoire, and on it is perched a beautiful silver frame with a picture of Nathanial that I took that first day inphoto shop. The other side of the room is a walk-in-closet and private bath. Just to the side, two small steps lead to my private reading room that boasts a small octagon-shaped window and a small scrapbooking area covered with photo albums, papers, stickers, and so on. Open on my table is my newest project, pictures of Nathanial from our first day.

In typical man fashion, he starts admiring my top-of-the-line electronics and massive music and DVD collections. We both crawl on the bed with a notepad in hand and flip on the TV.

"*Groundhog Day?* I love this movie. It's a classic," I say. He agrees, and we both laugh.

We pile the pillows to prop us up a little, get comfy, and began our guest list, starting with the most obvious first:

ELIJAH AND FLORENCE
ISAAC AND CONSTANCE
ALEXANDER AND MATILDA
NATHANIAL AND SOPHIA
"That looks really good together," Nathanial admits.
ARTHUR AND NIKOLE MCCORD
LUKE MCCORD
MATT BARTON AND EBONY TRIGGS
ELIZA TRIGGS
MS. EDWINA TRIGGS
BEN (FROM FOOTBALL)
MR. WILSON
MRS. HUNT

We will need to get a list of those from the hospital that Constance and Isaac will want to invite, also you need to do one for your buddy's from football. The invite will include all of their families as well. Now that we have the guest list ready, we can work on the invitation layout. We don't have much time to plan, as Christmas is just days away, which means New Years is just over a week away and most people probably have plans already.

We work on making up invitations on my Mac and decide to hand deliver them. We play around with a few of the programs on my computer until we find one we like. After trying various fonts, colors, and background patterns, we decide a classy and formal look is the way to go.

"Okay. I think we can print these off now," I announce.

"Yeah, I think they look great," Nathanial replies.

Happy New Year!
Please help us celebrate our first
New Years in Wenham.
at the Pierce family residence
182 Mountain Drive
Six p.m. on December 31
Bring the entire family for
dinner, refreshments, and entertainment.
Children's room and nanny on hand.

After printing we add ribbons to them, making them as elegant as we can for homemade invitations, before taking them downstairs to show the rest of the family.

"They are really quite lovely. I adore the steel blue paper with the silver ribbon," Florence admires.

"Thanks. We'll add some snowflake and champagne glass confetti and then seal the envelopes with our family seal in red wax,"

Nathanial grabs a small basket sitting next to the sofa filled with magazines. "Can we use this to carry the invites in?"

"Yeah, sure. That will work nicely," I reply.

"Cool. Sounds like a plan." he says with one of his killer smiles.

Chapter Thirty Five
The Park

We start to organize the invites in the basket according to address. We have quite a few families to deliver to.

"We should get going and deliver these before it gets too late," I suggest.

"It may take us a while. We are lucky everyone lives fairly close to one another." Nathanial picks up the basket and grabs my hand, leading me out of the room.

I see the rest of my family is busy preparing, so I just tell Alexander we are going to deliver the invites. I am actually a little excited. My family has hosted lavish parties before, but never one with so many mortals. This should prove to be an interesting and new experience for us all.

◆ ◆ ◆

Nathanial and I drive to the school end of town. This will be the best place to start, and we can just walk the streets of the area delivering our invitations. It is a nice evening out, with a slight chill in the air and tiny perfect snowflakes falling from the sky above. Wenham is such a scenic town. It is not as modern as most places are. In the center of the town park, there is a magnificent gazebo with white lights hanging from the roof. The biggest poinsettias I have ever seen line the path from the street and surround the gazebo.

Everything about this town feels like home and welcoming. The sun is setting and it is striking.

Nathanial and I both stand frozen as we look down the pathway into the park. It is the same park where he was attacked about a week ago. I look up at Nathanial as he squeezes my hand just a little tighter. "Are you alright? We can go another way," I suggest.

"I am fine. Don't worry about me. It is just now that I know the truth, and I see the entire attack a whole new way-the right way, just like it happened. I can actually remember it all and see what I never saw before," he explains as if he is watching it happen. "I look over to where we were and I can picture the vampire ready to attack. Now I can see Alexander and Mati heading toward us at incredible speeds."

"Don't do this to yourself," I insist.

"Do you see that? There is a man over there behind the tree." Nathanial stands tall and tries to shield me just as he did the night of the attack.

"Oh my God! I don't believe it." If I could have gone any paler, I would have.

"So you see him too?"

"No. I see my brother."

"Alexander? What is he doing here?"

"No, it's Caspian. He is here."

"Well don't just stand here. Go! I will wait for you."

I take a few steps forward and just speak aloud. I do not want to scare him away. "Caspian, I know it's you, and you can come home. We miss you, and you are always welcome back." I watch as he turns and disappears into the night once again. "Caspian...NO! Please don't leave again!" I shout, to no avail.

Once in a while, I swear I see Caspian. I know he likes to keep tabs on where we are staying. I always hope he comes home to us soon. This has been the closest he has gotten. I have never been able to speak to him like today. Maybe the day of Caspian's return is nearing. I now know the entire family wishes for him to come back to us. Caspian making his presence known to me may be something for my family to look into. This is twice in a week that a member of our family has spotted him. I wonder why he is getting closer, and I hope it is because he plans on returning to us soon.

"Are you okay, Sophia?" Nathanial wraps his arm around me.

"Yeah, thanks. It is just so awkward for him to show up now, when my family and I have been discussing finding him. We actually started talking about it since your attack, and to see him here where the attack happened is odd. Alexander believes he was here that night too." I rest my head on Nathanial's chest as he holds me.

"That is a little weird, quite the coincidence. Can you tell me more about him?"

"Caspian was great. Aside from the bond Alexander and I have, Caspian was dearest to me. I have always turned to him whenever I needed something. Everyone has always treated me like some fragile little girl, but not him–not Caspian. He was always honest with me. Caspian would share things with me no one else would. He is a few hundred years older than I am and lived like a true vampire for most of that time. He was only able to go out at night. He hunted and fed off humans to stay strong. But Caspian was tired of living like that. He was a perfect fit for our family," I explain.

"Yeah, the story you told me about Caspian explains so much, especially why you were so reluctant to get involved with me now. Don't worry, honey. That will never happen to us. I believe in you and know that you are stronger than that," Nathanial comforts.

"I was not sure if I could resist you. Your scent overpowered me for the longest time. It was all I could think about," I admit.

"And has that changed?" he questions.

"Yes. You still appeal to me, but ever since the attack, I've had the advantage of knowing I can control it. With the open wound and your blood spilling all over me that night, your scent is imprinted in me. I know now without a doubt that I can resist the temptation of your blood," I say with pride.

We begin to walk further up the path hand in hand, and Nathanial asks, "Do you think Caspian will rejoin your family?"

"Well, we can't worry about it now. We have a job to do." I begin to lead the way to our next delivery.

It is so much fun running up and down the streets and placing the invites in the doors. I pick up a little of the snow that has fallen to the ground from a large spruce tree towering above us. As I walk toward Nathanial, I slowly reach up and tuck the snow down the back of his shirt.

He begins doing a funky chicken dance, hopping around to try and get it out. "You'll pay for that." He grabs a handful of snow and starts chasing me down the street.

It feels so good to laugh uncontrollably. I lean over the bus stop bench as Nathanial comes up behind me. Grabbing my waist, he picks me up, and a moment later there I am lying on the snow-covered grass. Nathanial falls beside me, and we roll around together, laughing as we play in the white stuff like little kids on a snow day. *This is so much fun*, I think to myself. *Everything about this feels so real, so normal.*

How is it possible that someone like me is so lucky? To be able to find such happiness–even something that resembles happiness–is a grand feat for my kind. This is unbelievable.

"We better stop horsing around and finish these deliveries," I say with a giggle.

"Yeah, I think you are right. The next house is just over there." He points down the street.

Nathanial and I are just about finished delivering the invites to everyone, and then it hits us: Christmas is in two days.

"Oh my gosh. I need to finish my shopping." I explain.

Chapter Thirty Six
Shopping

Nathanial and I head over to the mall. We pick out a few things for our families and a few close friends. I am enjoying myself, just walking around the mall like two teens in love do. We do a little window shopping, and we even run in to a few of Nathanial's friends. It is nice to feel part of something after so many years. Being that we do not know each other's families too well yet, we decide to purchase gifts from both of us as a couple. I pick out gifts for my family, and he picks out presents for his. I encourage him to get his parents something really nice, something they would never expect.

"I don't think I have ever gotten my shopping done that fast before. You are a shopping machine," Nathanial jokes.

With a little chuckle, I respond, "I've had a little practice."

We finish our shopping, we decide to head back to the house and wrap the newly purchased gifts.

"Maybe we should pick up some wrapping paper and ribbon before we leave the mall," I suggest, remembering that we don't have wrapping supplies at home.

"That may help a little," he agrees with a chuckle as we head back into the mall.

◆ ◆ ◆

"Sophia, these look too nice to open," Nathanial compliments.

"I perfected my wrapping skills a little while ago," I joke.

We both have a good chuckle over it.

"I have a feeling you have perfected many things."

"Well, you know the saying. Practice makes perfect. With all the practice I have had, I'm near perfect at everything." I wink.

"The only point I will argue is that you aren't near perfect–you are completely perfect. That's just part of what I love about you." He leans in and kisses the corner of my mouth. When we finish wrapping all the packages, Nathanial says, "I need to talk to Alexander. I need him to help me with something."

"That's fine because I need to visit Ebony for a bit." I am sure she can help me find the perfect gift for Nathanial. Ebony and I made plans for a shopping trip, and boy am I in the mood for this one.

"Why don't you and Alexander do what you need to, and I'll head over to Ebony's for a while? Maybe Alexander can drive you home if I don't get back in time," I suggest.

"Sounds great, sweetie. Have fun. I love you and will see you later." He gives me a small kiss and heads toward Alexander's room; I hear the knock on Alexander's door.

I brush my teeth and grab a sweater. As I leave, I notice Alexander and Nathanial have moved into the office. They are deep in discussion and being very quiet. I try to hurry by, so as not to overhear what they're talking about. They pause and wave so I don't hear anything. They are acting very secretive, and I find myself wondering what they are up to. Easy enough, I brush it off and jump in my car to head to Ebony's house.

I drive the speed limit today. I am not in a hurry and just want to enjoy the scenery. The stores are open until midnight tonight for last chance shopping, so we have about four hours to find our guys the perfect gift. I arrive at the manor and walk up to the door.

Ebony is all ready to go.

"May I come in and say hello to everyone?"

"If they were here you could, but they are all shopping too," she answers.

"Typical women we are." I laugh.

We get back in the car and go out on our shopping mission. Once we arrive at the mall, we begin the hunt and talk as we look for bargains. Ebony and Matt have been getting closer. I am happy for her. In all my years, I have never had such a good friend. She is kind, caring, honest, sincere, and extremely loyal–not to mention a very talented witch. I really enjoy having a girlfriend to share things with. We have had a few slumber parties with our sisters–just the usual stuff like pedicures, manicures, and girl talk. It is so much fun, and it is nice to have others around besides just our family for a change.

"What on Earth are we going to get the boys?" I ask.

"I have no idea. We have been up and down this mall, and I can't think of anything. They are both so special. We have to get them the perfect gift," Ebony emphasizes.

"I got it!." I yell.

"What?" Ebony asks.

"We should get the guys something like a ring, a watch, or a wrist band, and then you can put a protection spell on it to ensure that others' powers can't influence them unless they allow them to with full understanding," I whisper.

"You are amazing. That is perfect. With all the craziness going on around here right now, I would feel better knowing our little mortal boys are protected," she agrees enthusiastically and reveals, "I have had a sense of evil approaching."

"What do you mean?" I inquire.

"I don't know. I just have this feeling that something bad is heading our way and we should be prepared," Ebony informs me. "You know; like something wicked this way comes."

"Let's discuss it with my family later and see if they know anything. But for now, let's go shopping." I grab her hand and pull her in my direction.

We start walking to the goldsmith shop. When we get there, the gentleman explains that he makes most of his jewelry by hand, with the exception of the watches, which he can custom order from a friend of his. Both Ebony and I find a few things we like. The store owner places all the items on a black velvet mat so we can have a closer look.

I decide on a nice watch. "I remember Nate telling me one day that he wants to own a collection of nice watches. What better time to start?" I decide. The watch has a silver wristband and a white face, and small emeralds mark each hour. It is perfect.

Ebony decides on a black leather wristband with an attached silver medallion that can be engraved. She chose to have his name put on it in a Celtic script since he is of Irish decent.

We stop at Starbucks, where Ebony gets cafe mocha and I enjoy a double espresso.

"I know the day crystal helps you digest human food, but why are you having coffee? I know you don't need it," Ebony inquires.

"Well a few things help to decrease vampire cravings, and caffeine is one of them. Plus, it's a great way to spend time with friends," I explain. "Besides, who can pass on Starbucks?"

Chapter Thirty Seven
Protection

When we arrive back at the manor, we notice that Ebony's sister and Grams are also back from shopping.

"We have a great idea for the boys' Christmas gifts," Ebony announces.

"Really? What?" Eliza questions.

"Because of everything that happened to Sophia and Nathanial at the winter formal, we were thinking of putting a protection spell on their gifts."

"Look. We picked out some great gifts for them. We tried to think of something they would keep with them at all times." I pull the gifts out of the bag and show the other ladies.

"Will you help us place a protection spell on these?" Ebony requests.

"Girls, this really is a great idea," Ms. Edwina says as she goes to the office. She returns with the *Book of Shadows*.

I'm so excited. This is working out great. If the two sisters do the protection spell together, it will be stronger because of the Triquetra. We begin looking through the *Book of Shadows* to find the proper spell, and it proves to be simpler than we had expected.

As I reach for the book, it slams shut and moves away from me. "Oh my God! That scared the crap out of me. What just happened?" I ask.

Mrs. Edwina smiles. "That is how a protection spell works. When a family creates their *Book of Shadows*, the first spell they usually use is a protection spell. It is placed on the book so that the book can never get in to the wrong hands. Only a blood relative or guardian can touch the book."

"What is a guardian?"

"They are the protectors of good witches, our own personal guardian angel."

"That is so cool. So no one else can ever touch the book?" I confirm.

"In most cases, no, but there are some occasions where another witch, a warlock, or even a demon finds a way to break the spell. That is why it is so important to keep the book safe. All our family secrets are in this book, and if the wrong entity gets a hold of it, they will be able to destroy our bloodline completely, not to mention wreaking all sorts of other havoc in the world," Mrs. Edwina warns.

"That is very interesting. I hope the protection spell for Nathanial and Matt works just as well."

"Grams, I never knew all that. I mean, you had mentioned something about protecting the book before, but never about it being protected and why," Ebony says with interest.

"There is so much for you girls to learn. I do not want to rush things and overwhelm you," Ms. Edwina replies.

"Thank you, Grams, but I think both Ebony and I want to learn it all. Finding out we are real witches was the biggest shock. Not much else could be more shocking or overwhelming," Eliza confirms.

"Oh just wait. The first time you have a meeting with a demon or some other evil supernatural being, you will be surprised. You always need to be prepared. They can show up anywhere and at anytime," Ms. Edwina lectures.

"Okay, Grams. We understand, but I think for now, we should try the spell," Ebony suggests.

"I am so excited to actually try a spell on something," Eliza admits.

"Okay, Sophia. May I please have the gifts?" Ms. Edwina holds her hands out.

I place the gifts in her hands. She turns and places them in the center of the room and surrounds them with four white candles, one at each of the four points of the Earth: north, south, east, and west.

"Okay. Now, Ebony and Eliza, I want one of you to stand to the east and one to the west sides of the gifts and candles and then start chanting the spell," Ms. Edwina instructs.

"By the dragon's light,
On this December night,
We call to thee, give me your might,
By the power within,
We conjure thee.
To protect all that,
We surround,
So mote it be,
So mote it be,
So mote it be!!!"

As they complete the spell, all the candles flicker and go out.

"That was so cool" I jump with excitement.

"That was pretty cool, and so much fun." Ebony runs to me, and we jump around in a circle with our arms locked like a couple of giddy young girls after their first date.

"We should test it out and make sure the spell worked," Eliza says as she puts each item on, one at a time.

Ebony tries to move items to hit her. My keys fly out of my hand directly at Eliza, but about a foot away from her, they just stop and fall to the ground. She tries a coffee mug from off the table. It flies through the air, and we all watch as it explodes in the same spot where the keys stopped. It is like a force field is surrounding her. Items just bounce away or break as soon as they come within about a foot or two from her. Ebony continues to try, and Eliza dances around.

"Na na na na boo bo... you can't hit me!" Eliza taunts her sister.

"Oh what are we, preschoolers again?" Ebony says.

"Just trying to have a little fun, sis. Come on and take your best shot."

"GIRLS! Enough! You have proven that the spell works, and all you are doing now is destroying my home," Ms. Edwina yells.

"Oh, Grams, I am so sorry, I was just having some fun, and I will clean this mess up," Ebony says with remorse.

"I know, girls. It is the excitement of actually seeing a spell work. Now why don't you celebrate and then clean up this mess." She gathers the book and slowly down the hall to return it to the office for safekeeping.

"You two are absolutely amazing." I declare with elation. "This is the most amazing thing I have ever seen."

"Yeah, that is so awesome. I can't believe we did that. I know we have been practicing and working on our magick, but I never expected anything like this," Eliza boasts.

"I cannot wait to see what else you can do. Remind me to stay on your good side," I encourage with a joke.

"Totally. I think I will start to study the *Book of Shadows* to see what else I can find," Ebony proclaims.

With the gifts now linked to a protection spell they are ready to keep the men we love safe. Ebony and I wrap them so I can head home. It is getting a little late, and I want to mention Ebony's bad feeling to my family. I also still have to tell them about seeing Caspian earlier tonight. "I should get home. I can't wait to tell my family about this and what we talked about, Ebony." I say my goodbyes and head back home, where there are many things to be discussed.

Chapter Thirty Eight
Staying

Back at the house, I notice white lights hanging in all the trees that line our driveway, all the way up to the house. I walk in and see the biggest Christmas tree I think has ever been in someone's home. It is standing beautifully in the family room, right next to the fireplace, perfectly placed in front of the huge bay window. Boxes of decorations are lying everywhere. Everyone appears hard at work decorating the house, hanging mistletoe and stringing garland throughout the huge house.

I see Nathanial sliding down the banister of the grand staircase, and he lands right in front of me. He opens his arms to me. "I think this entitles me to a kiss."

"What do you mean?" I question, with a slightly puzzled look.

He points just above my head, and I look up.

I am standing under a large bunch of mistletoe. I smile at Nathanial. "I guess it does," I answer.

With his arms around me, he dips me down and plants a big kiss on me, as if he were Fred Astaire. I giggle like a little girl. "Hey, sweetie. Did you enjoy your time with Ebony? How is she doing?" he inquires.

"She is well. We had a lot of fun. I got to hang out with her sister a little too."

I love it when he calls me "sweetie," his little nickname for me. It's so cute. Just seeing him makes me smile, but I really enjoy seeing him in my family's home, alone with my family, as if he really does belong.

"What time do I have to return you to your parents?" I ask.

"You don't. I called and explained that Alexander is helping me with something, and I am allowed to stay the night." He surprises me with a grin.

"Really?" I say with excitement.

"Yeah. They spoke with Elijah and agreed, once he assured them I would be in a room away from yours."

We all laugh.

"Cool, I get to keep you." I move back in to his arms.

"Only for forever." he whispers.

"You can't live forever," I said with a hint of suspicion and a dirty look toward Constance.

"I can if I become like you." He is very blunt.

"And how would your family feel about that? What would we tell them?" I ask.

"They would understand my decision. They are very supportive," he begins to appeal.

"What about all your plans? Don't forget about football, college, and well...life," I argue.

"Things always happen in life that can change a person's plans," he rebuts.

I decide it was not worth the argument and ask, "Can't we just enjoy things a bit before making any permanent life altering plans?"

"Don't get that pretty little head of yours in a knot. I am just playing with you. Alexander told me that would bother you. I am really just teasing. I am sorry. I am quite happy to allow the chips to fall where they may." He looks at Alexander, and they both snicker.

"What is...oh, never mind. I don't even want to know." I give Nathanial a kiss and go to put his gift in a safe place.

When I come back downstairs, I grab some ornaments and begin to help with the decorating. The stereo is playing all our Christmas favorites, and we are all dancing around singing and laughing.

Florence comes out of the kitchen and shouts, "I made some homemade eggnog with a little spiced rum, if anyone wants any."

We all enjoy a glass. Alcohol, in moderate amounts, is another thing that helps to curb our cravings, and everyone knows eggnog is a Christmas tradition. Thanks to our day crystals, we can partake in such traditions and formalities as Christmas dinner, and traditions are very important to our family.

Isaac decides to make a toast. "Here is to friends, family, home, and eternal love. Thanks to Nate, another of our family has found love and is complete."

"Cheers!" everyone shouts.

"So Sophia, on Christmas Eve, my family walks the streets of town and looks at all the lights and decorations. Would you be interested in joining us this year?" Nathanial requests with a glimmer in his eyes.

"I would love to. I was also hoping you could sneak over here on Christmas day for a little while," I request.

"I didn't really think about it. I just assumed we would be together on Christmas. I'm sure I can manage some time away," he states. "We usually get up and check to see what Santa has left us. Dad makes breakfast, and Mom preps for a huge dinner. We sit around and play games like football and such. Then we eat and the exchange our gifts. I am sure I can sneak out after breakfast."

"I was also hoping to spend the holidays together, but I did not want to be presumptuous," I explain.

Once we finish with the decorating, we finalize our plans for Christmas, and then Nathanial sneaks off with Alexander again. I don't know what to do with myself right now. I feel so giddy knowing that Nathanial is in the house. I just want to see him and hold him. I know I will get my chance in a while. I know when he's done doing whatever he's up to with Alexander; he'll come and find me. I think I'll wait in my room and have a little down time. Today was pretty busy, and I still have not had the chance to talk to the family about seeing Caspian and Ebony.

I throw in a DVD of The *Christmas Story*, hoping it will put me to sleep since I've seen it a hundred times. It is awkward sleeping so much, as I've always needed just a small amount of sleep, maybe ninety minutes a day. Lately, I have been resting more and more, maybe because I found what I was looking for and am completely at peace now. Normally, I spend my nights reading, writing, or learning something new. There is so much to do, so why waste it sleeping? I always joke that I can sleep when I am dead.

♦ ♦ ♦

A few hours later, I hear footsteps heading toward my room, followed by a light knock at the door. "May I come in?" Nathanial asks softly.

"No need to ask." I sit up and run my fingers through my hair, trying to comb it out a bit.

He walks over and sits on the bed next to me. He brushes my hair out of my face and gently kisses my forehead. "Sorry I woke you."

"No, I am glad you did. Are you and Alexander finished with whatever you were doing?"

"Yep, and you are not getting anything out of me," he snickers.

"Okay, I won't ask," I huff and fold my arms over my chest.

He lies back, and I snuggle right into his arms. I feel so safe and warm with him, like I am right where I belong.

Nathanial is asleep almost immediately, so I just cuddle up to him. I enjoy watching him sleep. He is so peaceful. I only wish I could see into his dreams. I lie wrapped in his warm embrace, enjoying the aroma that is coming from him. It is so intoxicating and tempting. I fully remember the scent from his stabbing and how bad I wanted him. His scent is imprinted in me now. I can imagine it and almost taste it, but it does not pain me any longer. I can easily get lost within the rich bouquet of Nathanial.

I need to get my mind off of his scent and just enjoy being in his arms with him next to me. I decide to pick up a book; closest to me is a compilation of Hemingway's work called *The Wild Years*. I recall that it was published posthumously. I always enjoy his work, as it speaks to me in a way others don't. I just finished reading *The Diary of a Young Girl* by Anne Frank. I think I like that one because I saw with my own eyes the horrible atrocities committed by the Nazis. I can understand what she went through and felt. I relax and enjoy reading my book while the only man I have ever loved sleeps peacefully next to me.

I finish my book and I snuggle in to Nathanial even closer. It feels so right, yet so wrong to be in his arms. I almost feel like it is wrong to be this happy, this in love. I know I don't deserve him, so I wonder how I am so blessed to have him in my life. I close my eyes and imagine what it would be like to be a mortal again.

In my mind's eye, I see Nathanial and me enjoying high school and then college together. After both of us get our post-secondary degrees, we move back to Wenham and find jobs. I imagine if I was mortal, we would then begin to plan our wedding. Nathanial would ask my father for my hand before proposing, and he would plan the most amazing proposal. A small smile comes across my face at the thought of what could have been if I were someone else, and I continue my daydream a little more. After the most amazing wedding and a tropical honeymoon, we come back and announce to our families that I am expecting. Nine months later, I give birth to a handsome little boy, who looks just like his father. As I imagine this perfect life for Nathanial and me, I feel my face become damp. I can feel the tears streaming down my face like never before. I have always wanted children, a little boy of my own, and I picture him being just as amazing as Nathanial.

I have to stop imagining what never will be. I will never be a mother and never have a happy ending. I am grateful for finding love with Nathanial, and I need to focus on now instead of a future that can exist. Christmas is nearing, and that is something I can be happy about, at least for a little while.

Chapter Thirty Nine
Traditions

It's Christmas Eve, and we have all been busy with party planning. "I think we have it all covered." I say to Matilda.

"I think you're right. Things are falling into place," she responds.

Nathanial got a ride home from Alexander earlier in the day; he wanted some time with his brother. I love how close his family is, especially since so many families today are too busy for one another. That's not how it is with the McCords. They always make time for family and friends.

♦ ♦ ♦

It is about seven o'clock, time to meet the McCords for a stroll down the streets, I am so honored that Nathanial and his family wants to include me. I make sure I drink before going, to avoid any problems. Everyone is ready to go when I arrive, so we start down the street immediately.

The houses are done up nicely. Every house in town decorated, and it is brilliant. Food bank donation boxes line the streets throughout the town, and they are overflowing.

"Thank you so much for inviting me. Is the town like this every year?" I ask, imagining this as a piece of heaven. The perfect man is holding me close, and his perfect family is guiding us through a perfect town during the most perfect season of the year.

"Yes, it is tradition for every household to decorate. The town holds a contest every year for the best-dressed house," Mrs. McCord explains.

"These are amazing. I have never seen a community put so much effort into decorating," I admit.

"Yes, the holidays are very important around here," Mrs. McCord replies.

I examine each and every house, and they are all different. Some have thousands of lights, while others have animated reindeer moving to synchronized music. This is so magical, and to experience it with such a wonderful family is a wonder all its own. My every Christmas wish is coming true.

"Sophia, I realize it is short notice, but we would love to have you and your family join us for dinner tomorrow," Mrs. McCord requests.

"I think that would be wonderful. You do know there are eight of us, right? I don't want it to be too much trouble."

"I love to cook. I could probably feed the entire block if I put my mind to it," she assures me, and everyone nods in agreement with goofy grins on their faces.

I let out a slight giggle and accept the kind holiday invitation on behalf of my family. "We shall be there then. Thank you so much for the invitation."

We continue around the neighborhood and make our way back to the McCord residence.

"Would you care to join us for some eggnog, Sophia?" Mrs. McCord invites.

"Yes, I would enjoy that. Thank you."

Inside the house, Mr. McCord starts a fire, as his wife pours the beverages. I assist her in serving.

"Thank you, Sophia. Your parents should be very proud of you. I believe you are a fine young woman," she compliments.

"I believe they are. Thank you again."

"Why don't you tell us a little more about yourself? Luke mentioned that you told him and Nate you were adopted from Italy?"

"Yes. Alexander, my twin brother, and I were adopted by the Pierce family years ago. We were a little older, so we still remember our biological family. We could not have asked for a better family to join though."

Nathanial's mother smiles. "May I ask what happened that they were able to adopt you?"

"Of course you may. Back in Italy, there was a terrible accident that made us available to the Pierces. We were very lucky they found us." My explanation holds truth, albeit lacking a little detail.

"I bet they believe they are the lucky ones." She pats my knee.

"So what about your family? What can you tell me about you?" I ask, trying to draw her attention away from my family.

"There really is nothing exciting about us. Arthur and I fell in love about twenty-five years ago. We had known of one another but never spoke until we had English class together." She smiles lovingly at her husband.

"She had me at hello," Mr. McCord says, and they both chuckle.

I wonder what is so funny. I think it is sweet.

"Dad, enough with the movie quotes." Nathanial shakes his head.

Luke smiles. "Sorry, Sophia. Our parents are movie freaks and can turn almost any conversation into some kind of script."

"Yes, I suppose they're right about that. In my defense, though, the moment I first heard that line, I knew it described how I felt and still feel about your mother."

"That is cute!" I smile at the dream of everlasting love.

◆ ◆ ◆

Christmas morning, Nathanial shows up just after breakfast as he promised. Luke drove him and left to go help his mother prepare for the evening dinner for twelve. I would have loved to introduce Luke to my family, but they will meet him tonight. I hold Nathanial's hand and lead him inside.

He seems to feel very comfortable here. "Merry Christmas, everyone," he announces.

"And to you as well, Nate" Florence returns the gesture.

A smile beams across my face as I watch the man I love walk to each member of my family and hug and kiss them. He really does belong with us and is the perfect fit.

Once the formalities are complete, Constance readies her camera. On the tripod stand she sets the timer to take a picture. "Okay, Nate. Time for one of our Christmas traditions. Every year, we gather in front of the tree and take a family picture."

"That sounds great. I will take the picture for you."

"Nate, we want you in the picture. You belong with us." Florence says, and with a evil look from me, "even if only for a short amount of time," She adds.

"Well, thanks. I am so glad you feel that way. I also believe I belong."

The entire family, along with Nathanial, stands in front of our tree, and we smile for our newest Christmas picture.

"Why doesn't everyone find a seat around the tree so we can open our gifts?" Florence suggests.

The entire family finds a spot. Matilda and Alexander sit side by side on the floor, as do Nathanial and I. The older members sit on the couch, and Danika is in front of the tree, ready to play Santa.

"Another tradition we have, Nathanial, is that the youngest member gets to play Santa and pass out all the gifts," Elijah explains.

"You must be relieved to pass on that tradition, Sophia. What? You did it for like a hundred years or something?" Nathanial asks.

"Yeah, something like that. I am glad to sit back and enjoy things a little more now."

"As much as I want to go first, you are our guest, Nate, so I guess you can start." Danika hands him the first gift. "This is from me."

Nathanial appears surprised that the entire family has gifts for him.

"You shouldn't be so surprised, Nate. We told you that you are part of this family now, and we exchange gifts in this family," Alexander explains.

He smiles and rips the paper off the box. A huge grin beams across his face as he pulls out a Patriots jersey and a certificate for name embroidering. "Thanks, Danika. This is so cool. How did you know I like the Pats?"

"Well, they are the closest football team to Salem, and you are a football nut. It was a lucky guess." She smile and winks at me.

"Yeah, I kinda am. Thanks so much. I love it," he says excitedly.

We all take turns opening gifts of clothing, jewelry, and so on. Matilda and Alexander give me the entire Nickelback

CD library so I can become more accustomed to Nathanial's favorite band. I get some really great gifts, but I think my best gift is Nathanial. I really do not need anything more. He is everything I could ever wish for. I look over my shoulder at the man sitting next to me, and I realize again that he is so perfect.

Nathanial is so elated as he opens his gift from Matilda and Alexander. "I can't believe you got me a designer pair of jeans, shirt, and this great sweater. It is way too much," he says as he puts the sweater on right away. He looks great in it, not that he needs the help, but the sweater suits him perfectly. "You have got to be kidding me." he screams. "Season tickets for the Patriots, plus the few games left for this season? I just can't believe it. This is amazing. Thank you, everyone." he screams as he begins to jump around like an over caffeinated monkey.

We nearly die of laughter.

"I think we did well!" Constance jokes.

"You did great! I can't wait to wear my new jersey to a live game."

"I told my family the New England Patriots is your favorite NFL team and that you have never seen a live game. I knew it would be something you would enjoy. They loved the idea, and we feel so bad that your football season ended early because of our kind."

"This is the best. Thank you again and again. It could not get any better."

"Well, Nate, you are not finished yet. This is from Elijah and Florence." Danika hands him a small box with a small green bow.

He opens it and looks confused. "It is a key, but for what?"

"The other part of your gift is over here. Follow me." Elijah leads Nathanial to the garage.

We all follow, and I hold Nathanial's hand, he has a puzzled look on his face and keeps looking at me with a questioning look. I just smile and say, "You'll see."

Once the door to the garage is opened and we are all inside, Florence flips the lights on and there, with a big green ribbon, is a shiny new Honda Insight just for him.

"Oh my God! This is way too much. I can't...you can't be serious. Your family has been way too generous already."

"But you can. We spoke with your parents, and they agreed to allow us to give this to you. You can't always borrow your mom's car, and you need to get to those Patriots games. We stretched the truth a little and explained that this is my car, but I do not like it and it is just sitting here. Now it's yours," Elijah insists and adds, "I suggested it would also be a good idea because of the distance between our houses, and I did not want Sophia to be driving you all the time, and being out late alone."

We all huff and chuckle at that.

"I don't know what to say. Thank you so much. This is unbelievable! I love the color, I don't think I have ever seen anything like it before." Nathanial is in complete shock, and we can all see it on his face.

"It is a pretty neat car. It is a hybrid, and the color is sky blue. We asked for green, but they don't offer that color, so this was the next best choice," Elijah says.

"It is great. Thank you. I just don't know what to say."

"Let's go back inside. You still have my gift to open." I tug at him after he does all the man things like looking under the hood and trying out the stereo.

Everyone heads back inside.

I stand in front of the gigantic spruce tree we decorated just a few nights earlier. I hold a small black box in my hands; it is wrapped with a red ribbon. "I found you less than four months ago, but I feel complete with you around. I want to protect you so that I can treasure you for every possible moment we have together." I smile and continue, "This gift is my way of keeping you safe." I hand him the box, lean in, and give him a small kiss.

He opens it slowly and looks at the contents carefully. "This is amazing! I love it. But I don't understand. How will a watch keep me safe?" Once again, he looks a little puzzled.

"Ebony and her sister put a protection spell on it. No supernatural power will be able to penetrate the protective field that surrounds you when you wear this, unless you willingly allow it to pass through," I explain.

"So Alexander can't read my mind now?"

"Not unless you want him to," I confirm.

Nathanial puts the watch on his left wrist.

"Okay, Alexander. Try it out." I order.

Alexander tries to see what Nathanial is thinking, and he trying to show him what he is thinking. The rest of us can see his frustration, and we laugh.

"Nothing. I can't get a thing." Alexander says with frustration.

"Okay. Now Nate, do you want him to see what you are thinking?" I suggest.

"There we go. I got it. Yeah, it is pretty cool," Alexander agrees with what Nathanial is thinking.

"Now just a second. I know you told me about witches, but Ebony?" Nathanial seems a little surprised.

"Sorry. Ebony and her sister are two of the most powerful witches in the world, but things shouldn't surprise you anymore. Anything is possible, and at this rate, I am not sure how much more you can take," I reply.

"Yeah, I am starting to see that now. It is all very surprising though. I guess all that talk about her around school is true then"

"Yes, it is all true, but some students paint her being a witch as a bad thing. Her family is very amazing, and I promise you will learn more about them soon."

He moves closer to me and gives me the sweetest, softest kiss ever. "This watch is amazing, just what I wanted. I love you, sweetie."

"I love you too!" I sneak another kiss.

"I guess it is time for your gift now." He smiles excitedly as he walks to the tree and pulls out a small box wrapped in shiny red paper.

I rip the paper off in excitement. I examine the small wooden box. It is the most beautiful thing I have ever seen. Two colors of wood blend together, intertwined like two folded hands, to make the creation. It looks handmade, sculpted from the finest wood. I can even smell the fresh woody scent of the timber. One side has our names engraved in to it: SOPHIA AND NATHANIAL. The other side two words perfectly inscribed: FOR ETERNITY. After admiring the box for a moment, I open the lid. Inside is a small red gem shaped like a heart, a ruby, placed delicately in the center of a white gold setting, just like my necklace and day crystal, but a ring. The gold wraps around into two half circles as if hugging the heart forming the setting of the ring. In the lid of the box is a small note that reads, "I give you my heart to have and protect. All my love, Nate." I am completely speechless. It is amazing, just like Nathanial.

"Alexander helped my vision come to life. May I help you put it on?" Nathanial asks.

I nod, and Nathanial takes the ring and places it on my left ring finger.

"This is my promise to you forever," he says with a smile.

"Nate, it is the most beautiful thing I have ever seen!"

"Then I guess you have never looked in a mirror."

"I love it, and I love you! Thank you so much."

Nathanial brushes the ring on my finger with his thumb and then brushes my cheek, running his fingers through my hair.

"I love you more than life itself." he whispers and leans in to kiss me.

I pull him closer for another. How could things get better than this? I now understand why people wait their whole lives to find that perfect one. It has taken me many lifetimes to find mine.

I am so caught up in the moment that the full meaning of the words Nathanial spoke, *"This is my promise to you of forever,"* didn't register in my mind at first, but now all I can think of is *only a vampire can love you forever.* I'm just so full of emotion, so full of happiness that I never experienced before nor ever thought I would. Moving to Wenham has fulfilled every dream I've ever had. I have a great best friend, the most incredible man ever, and accepting family members on both sides. Who could ask for more?

Chapter Forty
Bonding

It's only two o'clock, and it's already the best Christmas ever. Nathanial and I pack up all the gifts for his family and place them in the trunk of his new car.

"I can't wait to show my brother everything. He is going to be so jealous. I got all this great stuff, and the best part is I got the girl."

"I think our families will enjoy each other," I assume.

"Who couldn't love your family? Plus, this is just the first of many more celebrations together." He seems so enthusiastic.

My family brings some gifts for the McCord family and some wine to go with dinner. Both families greet each other with open arms.

"Please come in. Thank you for joining us," Mrs. McCord says. "My name is Nikole. This is my husband Arthur and our eldest son Luke. It is a pleasure to meet the family of the young girl who has stolen my son's heart."

Nathanial grabs Luke and they head outside to check out his new car. "Dude, you have got to see this." The rest of us kids join them. Alexander begins telling them all the vehicle specs and all the car talk. The adults stay inside to become acquainted with one another. Although I notice them peeking outside at us from time to time with smiles on their faces.

"I don't believe this. Are you sure you don't have an older sister for me? How about it, Mati? Want to go out on a date?" Luke jokes.

"I would be honored, but I am spoken for!" She winks at Alexander.

"Yeah, I know. I am just teasing, Nate told me you and Alexander are a couple and not actually siblings. Alexander, you are a lucky man."

"Yeah, I am. Thanks, man." Alexander pats Luke on the shoulder, and Nathanial shakes his head.

"Bro, you are such a player!" Nathanial punches Luke in the shoulder.

"No, man. I am just jealous. I would give anything to find the right girl. Don't get me wrong, I have had fun, but you found what Mom and Dad have, and I can only hope I will find it someday too," Luke admits, hopping into the passenger seat.

"You will. I can feel it. You have a great soul." Matilda offers.

"So are you gonna let me take it for a test drive?" Luke requests.

"Sure. Why don't you go with Alexander? He can tell you all about it! We'll wait out here for you to go around the block," Nate agrees.

"The block? I want to open this puppy up."

"Another day. It's Christmas, and we have guests!" Nate argues.

"So right, little brother. Excuse my rudeness," Luke agrees, and the two older brothers leave for a quick test drive.

While waiting for them to return, I can overhear the conversation going on inside the house.

"Florence, Elijah, it is way too much. We will never be able to repay you for the car," Arthur says.

"There is no need to worry. Our family is extremely privileged, and we enjoy sharing with those who come into our lives. This is a gift from our family, and if there is anything you need, please do not hesitate to ask. Sophia is happier than we have ever seen her. She has come out of her shell, and it is all thanks to your son. We can never repay you for that," Elijah insists. "Our families are now joined by love, and to us, that is as good as blood," he adds.

"Thank you. Our children have fallen fast for each other, but we believe it to be true, Nikole and I fell in love at first sight and have been together ever since," Arthur admits.

"We completely agree. It has all happened very fast, but we believe in true love as well. Our kids are soul mates, meant to be together, and it will only improve with our support," Elijah encourages.

Constance and Florence help Mrs. McCord put the finishing touches on dinner. By the time they finish, every counter in the kitchen, as well as the table, is filled with delicious-smelling food.

"Please fill your plates and have a seat wherever you can find room. It is a little snug, but try to make yourselves comfortable," Nikole encourages.

I love this, even more perfection to the perfect day, I think as I take a seat next to Nate on the floor in the family room.

We enjoy the evening, opening yet more gifts, talking, and playing games. I will remember this day for all eternity. Not only do I love Nathanial, but I am falling in love with his family almost as fast as I did with him. Our two families seem to fit so nicely together, I hope to have at least a few more Christmases like this before having to move on.

"Thank you so much for a beautiful evening. I trust you will all be joining us for New Years?" Isaac asks.

"Yes of course. We would not miss it. Is there anything we can do to help?" Nikole responds.

"Not at all. Just the pleasure of your company again will be enough. Please do not hesitate to bring any guests of your own. We have more than enough room and would enjoy meeting any of the townspeople," Constance adds.

Nathanial and I just look at one another without saying a word. I know we share the same thought: elation that our families fit so well together. I am now not only protective of Nathanial, but also of his entire family, and they all mean so much to me. It is very overwhelming. To fall in love at first sight with my soul mate was one thing, but his family is even more unexpected!

We exchange hugs with the McCord family and thank them again for a wonderful evening.

Nathanial sees us to our cars. "I promise to be over in the morning to finish with the party plans." He reaches out to me, and we share a small kiss. "Sweet dreams, my love." He closes the car door, only to stand and watch us drive away.

Back at home, my family raves about the wonderful family we just got to know. I think this could be a wonderful union between mortal and immortal. *This may work out better than I ever expected,* I thought to myself.

Chapter Forty One
Revisiting

We are having a little down time, and I think maybe this is the right time to talk to my family about Caspian again. I just don't know how to bring him up. It has only been a week or so since the last time I spoke to them about him and how I want to find him.

"What about Caspian?"

"Alexander! Sometimes I really hate it when you do that. You do know that don't you?"

"Sorry. I can't help it."

"What is it, though, Sophia? What about Caspian? We know he has been on your mind lately," Florence asks.

"I have wanted to tell you for a few days now. Nathanial and I saw Caspian in the park the other night when we here delivering the New Year's party invitations," I begin to explain.

"What do you mean you saw him?" Constance questions.

"Caspian was the in the park, close enough for me to know without a doubt that it was him. I called to him, but he ran off. He is here. Caspian is in Wenham!" I announce excitedly.

"He's here? He came back?" Matilda shouts.

"I didn't see this! I must not be connected to him anymore. He has been gone too long. Maybe, if I had touched something that was his." Constance lowers her head with disappointment.

"Constance, you can't see it all. Don't beat yourself up over it. Let's leave his return up to him," Isaac wisely suggests.

"So he ran off when you called to him?" Elijah confirms.

"Yes. I started toward him and called his name. He turned and ran into the woods." I explain.

"Well, we will have to keep an eye out for him. This is the closest he has gotten. Maybe he is as ready to come home as we are to have him home. That said, I do not want to push him." Elijah reaches for my hand to comfort me.

"That's it? We just watch for him?" I question.

"My dear that is all we can do. It is up to him when he comes home. All we can do is make it known that he is welcome back," Florence adds.

"What if I try to approach him? He doesn't know me and might not run off," Danika suggests.

"That may work, but I still do not want to push him. If he is watching us, I am sure he's aware that you are a member of this family. That may intimidate him more, since he does not know you," Elijah explains.

"I understand. I just want to help. I hate seeing the sadness it brings you to not have him here," Danika says, showing some understanding.

I'm shocked that Danika wants to help us. She is becoming a more trustworthy member of the family. Still, I have that odd gut feeling about her, as if something is amiss. My feelings for her are just as torn as they were for Nathanial before I let him in.

Alexander interrupts my thoughts, privately between us. "I can feel how concerned you are about Danika, but she really hasn't done anything to warrant your concern."

"I understand that. It's just a feeling I've always had, like she is going to be trouble for our family."

"Sophia, we're all here to support her, and she has been very successful so far. Just try to forget about it. I will keep an eye on her."

"Okay. I'll try."

"What secrets are you two sharing?" Matilda jokes.

"Just talking about how bad your hair looks tonight," I answer with a smile.

"What? Are you kidding?" Matilda jumps out of her seat and runs to the restroom to check, then yells, "You're so funny, Sophia. I'm gonna get you for that."

The entire family bursts out laughing. Poor Matilda thought she did not look perfect for a moment.

We continue to speak about Caspian for a while and decide there's not much more we can do.

Alexander adds, "I will try to connect with him so he knows he is welcome."

"And I will try to search my visions for him some more," Constance announces.

After we finish, I go to my room and listen to my new music collection. Sitting in the chair in my room with my legs draped over the arm, I start to relax. I could sit here for hours, thinking about my brother and admiring my new ring. It is so beautiful, just like what Nathanial and I share. I think this is the best Christmas I have ever had. At the very least, this is more meaningful than any past Christmases. After over a century, I finally feel at peace, and this feeling confuses me. I'm meant to be tormented for the rest of eternity. I guess that will come when I finally lose Nathanial.

I can't think of that. I need to enjoy this feeling while I still can. Today, I'm the luckiest being on Earth.

Chapter Forty Two
New Years

The day we have been planning for is finally here. It is time for our big New Years Eve party. Everything looks excellent. The decorations are amazing. We added fresh white roses around the house. The family ensures the finishing touches are complete, and Florence even added a WELCOME mat to the front step. The kitchen is filled with enough food to feed all of New England. We even have kid-friendly food for all the little ones that might be joining us. The hired staff members are starting to arrive, from a bartender and wait staff to the nanny and clowns for the kids. The DJ begins setting up in the family room, and the valets are outside, ready to park the cars.

As I peer out my bedroom window, I notice Nathanial and his family are the first to arrive. Everyone is dressed so dazzling. I've just finished dressing and start walking down the grand staircase toward Nathanial. I am wearing the cocktail dress Matilda gave me for Christmas. The white bustier and black above-the-knee skirt with crinoline is very retro! I finished it with a black pashmina and black heels. The low ponytail I have in my hair is tickling my back, and I smile. I feel stunning.

By the look on Nathanial's face, my guess is that he's in full agreement. My guess is confirmed when he says, "Well there is the most beautiful woman I have ever seen!" Nathanial smiles, and his brother and father both nudge him in my direction, as if he was frozen in place.

"Now this party is going to be fun. I am glad you are here." I greet my love with a kiss and proceed to his family. I smooch each one of them on the cheek. "I'm happy you could all make it. Please come in."

"Thank you so much for inviting us. You have a marvelous home," Mrs. McCord replies.

"It would not be the same without you," Florence interjects.

"May I help you with anything?" Nikole offers.

"I would love it if you help me have a good time. We have finished everything, and the staff will take care of the rest." Florence smiles.

Our guests are beginning to arrive. The house is filling quickly with the town residents, and everyone is mingling, telling each other about their Christmas. The wait staff is busy serving drinks from the bar, including any kind of cocktails, beer, champagne, juice, soda, and Shirley Temples that someone might want to order. Everyone will be taken care of and able to enjoy the party.

This is a great opportunity to meet and get to know the townspeople, especially since there are over a hundred guests. I'm enjoying talking with some of Nathanial's friends from football and school, along with their girlfriends. I glance around to see what my family members are all doing. Constance and Isaac are visiting with coworkers, and Florence and Elijah are meeting all the parents. Everything is going great. People are dancing to the music, and the kids are enjoying all the crafts and games we have set up for them. It seems to be a typical mortal party.

Nathanial starts to introduce my siblings and me to the students from school that made it to the party. Over the past weeks, we had met a few, but no one really wanted to interrupt us at the lunch table at school. We have a tight group the six of us along with Danika, and she is always around somewhere, which isn't too bad. I'm beginning to feel like I am truly experiencing high school for the first time. I am even able to talk to some of the football team members and their girlfriends; they are a lot less judgmental than I first assumed.

Ebony and Matt finally arrive and join in on the conversation.

"Hey, Ebony! I am so glad you are here," I say with a hug.

"Hi, Ebony," a few of the girls say. I am glad we didn't invite Mel; the girl Ebony had the run-in with at school. I would have ended up ripping what she has of a heart out of her chest.

"Hey, everyone! How are things going, Sophia? Sorry, but we got a little held up. Eliza had an outfit meltdown," Ebony explains with a chuckle.

"Well, she looks great. Crisis averted, I see." I wink at her.

A group of us head to the dance floor and start dancing the night away, laughing and having fun without a care in the world. The DJ is playing an array of music, but everyone seems to really get into things once he starts to play the top hits from the eighties. Who doesn't love Duran Duran and Michael Jackson?

Some of the girls from school notice my ring that Nathanial strategically placed on my left hand ring finger, causing more than a few questions.

"Oh my! Your ring is beautiful! Is it from Nate?" asks a pretty, petite girl whose name I don't recall.

"Yes. It was my Christmas gift. It really is lovely, isn't it?" I reply.

A girl named Paige, who I remember as the girlfriend of one of the football players, asks, "Wow! Does it mean—?"

I stop her mid sentence. "It's just a gift from my boyfriend that I am wearing on my ring finger, it even matches my necklace." I point out.

"Sorry. We didn't intend to pry."

"You did, but it is alright, and I'm sorry for my rudeness!" And we giggle.

Everyone is warming up to me, and I am warming up to them as well. I will admit there is more than one teenage girl whose head I'd love to rip off. I can hear a few of them whispering and such. I guess I'm no different than other high school girls, and we can't all get along. It's getting more and more like real life every day.

"Are you alright, Sophia? You look like you could use a drink," Nathanial says.

"I think you're right. Please excuse me for a moment."

"Do you mind if I join you?" Nathanial politely requests.

"Hey, can I come too?" Ebony asks.

"Sure, I...um, I guess so," I agree reluctantly.

I lead the two downstairs to the cellar, where we have a hidden room to store all our blood products.

"Why is it you keep all food, per se, down here?" Ebony asks.

"We only moved our supplies to this room because of the party. We did not want any wondering eyes finding it," I reply.

"Your family thinks of everything," Nathanial says with a chuckle.

"So Nate, I am just curious, how did you know I needed to get away and have a snack?"

"I could feel the frustration you're feeling, and I know every laugh line and freckle on your face. When I saw your eyes turn a darker shade of green, I knew it was time to get you out of there."

Ebony holds up a bottle. "Is this the one you need, Sophia, from the juice jug?"

"Yeah. Just a small glass would be great. Are you both sure you want to stay here? Neither of you have seen me feed or drink before," I say nervously.

"Really, how bad can it be? We pour you a glass, and you drink it like any other beverage," Ebony says with a hint of sarcasm.

"It is not really that simple. If I am able to control the features like my fangs and eyes with the smell, once I taste the blood, I will not be able to control it anymore. Are you sure you are both ready to see me...the real me?"

"Sweetie, we know the real you and look at the real you every day," my beloved reassures.

With a slight reluctance, I take the glass of blood that Ebony pours for me. I turn my head away from the two of them and take a small sip. I feel the ache as my fangs come out and the burn of my eyes as they go black.

Nathanial turns my head back to them. "Sweetie, please. You don't need to be ashamed, and we accept you for everything you are. We are bound to see this more than once in a while, and I must say you look beautiful."

I quickly finish the rest of my drink and relax myself to return to the party. I slip in to the restroom and brush my teeth.

"I just want to thank you both for being so supportive of me. I could never ask for better people around me than the two of you. I love you both. Are you sure you can both handle seeing me like that?'

"Nate is right, Sophia. We are fine. We are here for you, which is why we came with you. Now let's get back to the party."

They both put their arms around my shoulders, and we returned to the festivities and celebrations once I relax enough and my features return to normal.

Chapter Forty Three
Tribulations

Ebony and I continue dancing the night away and making a few new friends until Alexander summons us to the library telepathically. He also asks for Ebony and her sister to join us. I'm concerned that this must be something big to call us away from the party. We sneak in one by one, trying to be discreet. Constance and Alexander are intent in their conversation, and it looks serious.

"What happened?" Isaac inquires.

"Alexander, Constance, we are all here. What is it?" Elijah demands to know.

Constance begins, "I was outside for some air and went for a quick run. I brushed by a tree and started having a vision that Alexander intercepted. It is bad, real bad! The decedents of the Cerberus cult have risen from their lairs in the wastelands and are on the hunt. Many mortals have been killed in the New York area, and they have moved south to the Boston area. This could turn into another war, a repeat of Tansy the Vampire War when the groups took sides." She looks terrified.

"I think we need to be careful. We should also contact the Renata leaders to notify them of the Cerberus presence," Isaac adds.

We all agree. Elijah and Isaac will stay behind to discuss the details, and the rest of us will return to the party. We do not all want to be absent at the same time or it may look suspicious. We will discuss everything after the party.

"I'm confused. What is the Tansy, Renata and the Cerberus?" Eliza asks.

"Back in the fifth century, a war called Tansy broke out, separating the vampiric clans. A group came together to create an organization called the Renata. They suppressed the anarchs and agreed to exist behind a façade called 'The conspiracy of silence.' The leaders, or 'Lords', of the Renata decreed 'Never more shall vampires kill freely and openly, and they must hide amongst the mortals and conceal our true natures," Elijah explains and adds, "Thus came the six laws, a sort of Vampire Bible. Those who did not join the Renata were driven into the wastelands–that is, until they attacked the leaders for power, most recently, in 1882, when the vampire riots broke in New York and their numbers decreased once again. The Cerberus went into hiding again so as to increase their numbers. Because of the similarities to the original war, these riots are referred to as the 'Wars of Tansy.'"

"Well okay then. I guess that explains a little, where is this Renata located are they worldwide or just here?" Eliza says with a little surprise.

"They are from Transylvania; you know some of the myths about us are real." Isaac chuckles.

"Okay that is kinda funny but on the same note this might explain the bad feeling I have been having," Ebony suggests.

"What bad feeling?" Elijah asks.

"I have had this awful feeling that something bad was going to happen, something evil. I told Sophia about it the other night when we went shopping."

"Did I forget to mention it? Maybe seeing Caspian that night just overwhelmed me and took precedence. I am so sorry."

"No worries. We know now and need to figure out some details. Knowing last week without any details would not have meant much. Now we know to trust Ebony's feelings, as they may have more to them," Elijah says in his comforting voice.

We need to hide our concerns for now and continue with our own façade, starting with returning to the party. It is almost midnight now, and everyone is preparing to ring in the New Year. The wait staff assures us that our guests all have champagne, with sparkling cider for the underaged guests.

The music stops, and everyone gathers around for the countdown."Ten...nine...eight...seven...six...five...four...three...two...one... HAPPY NEW YEAR!" Balloons, streamers and confetti fall from the ceiling above, right on cue; Constance rigged it perfectly to fall in sync with the clock striking twelve. Everyone in attendance starts shouting, cheering, and singing off-key versions of "Auld Lang Syne." Then each guest turns to kiss the one they wish to spend the next year with. Of course Alexander and Matilda are hiding around the corner for a small kiss; they don't want to raise any questions.

This tradition means so much more to me now. I have waited over a century to find someone special, someone worth a New Years kiss. I never expected to find him, and for once I feel extremely lucky, standing here in the moment of a new year, with the most amazing man I have ever known and completely in love. Nathanial takes me in his arms, and we kiss, sharing the perfection of the moment.

"Sophia, let's go upstairs for some privacy and to talk. The party is winding down, and I don't think anyone will notice us missing." He knows me so well that he can tell something is bothering me.

"I think you're right. Let's go."

Chapter Forty Four
Connections

"So I think the party is a success. What do you think?" Nathanial inquires.

"Yes, it is all very nice. I enjoyed meeting your friends instead of them just gawking at us," I reply.

"So what is going on? You seem preoccupied," he inquires with genuine concern.

"You can tell?" I ask.

"I feel like we have known each other forever, and I can sense when something is bothering you, I told you so earlier. Relax and tell me what is going on and what I can do to make it go away, sweetie." He places his arm around my shoulder and gives me a little squeeze.

"I will, but tonight is not the night. Let's enjoy our first New Year's celebration together. I promise to tell you later," I insist. I make an X over my heart with my index finger and smile.

"Alright, but only because you are so breathtaking that I can't possibly argue with you," he says with his goofy little crooked grin that I so adore.

"So then why don't you come closer and give me another kiss?" He pulls me closer, and I allow it.

He pulls me right onto his lap. Now up on my knees with one on either side of his lap, straddling him. I begin pressing my hands against his perfectly shaped pectorals and lean in closer. I kiss his soft, gentle lips. Our lips moving together in perfect sync, becoming more and more passionate. He softly runs his hands down my sides and rests them on my hips. Things are getting intense. I have never felt passion like this before. It is obvious we have both forgotten about the house full of guests. It is as though only the two of us exist. Nathanial's hands move around the back of my hips, gently caressing my buttocks. I press in even closer, and he grabs even harder. He turns me so that my back is flat on the couch and he's half on top of me. Still kissing, I never imagined passion like this existed.

Just then, we hear a knock at the door, and we both jump to our feet. I answer the door, and it is Luke.

"Hey, bro. Sorry to interrupt, but Mom and Dad are ready to go. Can I catch a ride home with you? I'm kinda digging this girl named Eliza." He winks at Nathanial.

"Sure, no problem. Whenever you are ready." He laughs.

The three of us go back downstairs and say our goodbyes. This is yet another amazing evening spent with Nathanial McCord that I shall never forget! I'm so excited to see what the following months shall bring us. I only hope it is half as good as Christmas and New Years has been. *This is better than any dream or movie*, I think to myself. I know it's not movie though, because this will not have a happy ending, but for now, I've decided to just go with it and enjoy it while I can. I don't ever want this to end, but I do not ever want anything to harm Nathanial. I vow to protect him for as long as I am near, for as long as he will allow me continue to be a part of his life.

♦ ♦ ♦

"Luke and Eliza really are growing close. They have been talking for hours," Nathanial notes.

"I know. Everyone else has left. They're locked eye to eye and don't even notice the cleaning crew working around them," I reply.

Matilda gives me a look that I know; they have a special bond. I only wonder if things can continue to grow once Luke returns to school this week.

"I've never seen my brother this interested in anyone before."

"Do you think it could go somewhere? Mati believes they are a perfect match," I whisper.

"It could. Luke is very dedicated to everything he's passionate about, and he looks pretty passionate to me."

I watch the two kindred spirits bond. "I hope he can handle her secret as well as you've handled mine."

"I think he will. Mom and Dad always raised us to not judge others based on their circumstances, race, or beliefs. Luke is the fairest person I know, always ready to stand up for the outcast."

After a little longer, Nathanial interrupts Luke and Eliza's conversation. "Luke, I'm sorry, man, but even the staff has left. I think it may be time to let Eliza go home with her sister. I bet Mom and Dad are wondering what's taking us so long."

"You're probably right." Luke turns back to Eliza. "I am so glad we met tonight. I hope we can spend more time together before I go back to school."

"I would like that. Thank you for keeping me company." Eliza smiles and Luke leans in for a small kiss on the cheek before leaving.

The boys are the last of the mortals to leave. The family invites the sisters to stay and brush up on our vampire history. We get our journals out and look for all notes regarding the Cerberus.

Elijah has spent most of the night researching the murders from the New York area and trying to figure out which ones and how many could be attributed to the Cerberus. He also spoke at length to the Renata. Elijah has agreed to work with them to keep the peace and protect the secret. He explains to us, "Isaac, Florence, Constance, and I have faced them before in the previous New York riots, before we found you kids. When we found you, everything changed for us. We were living differently than most of our kind, but with you came responsibilities. You have heard some of the stories, but you have never been involved firsthand before. This is not the kind of fight our family is used to. Our fights are usually within ourselves, fighting our natural urges to feed off the mortals. Our biggest fight has always been our civility. Now we were opening up things that have been dormant in us for over a century. We must all be prepared."

We all agree that something needs to be done to stop the Cerberus; for human sacrifice is not something we can just sit idly by and watch. We've only been in Wenham for less than six months but have never had such a life before. We have never found so many mortals to care about. The townspeople are not only the civilians of Wenham, but they are also our friends, and some are like family to us.

We decide in this moment that it's not an option to allow the Cerberus to come anywhere near Wenham on their killing spree. We know the only option is to prepare for battle, fight them, and win. This will be difficult and training needs to begin immediately. We'll need help, but we may not be lucky enough to find it. When things become difficult like this is when I miss Caspian the most. He was always a great fighter and protector. I can feel our entire family longing for him now. I possibly yearn for his return even more since I saw him in the area only a few short days ago. I just don't believe anything can bring him back, not even the danger that is upon his family. We are his family and will always be. I hope one day soon he will realize we can help him and that he will join us again.

"We must begin training and preparing. I think Danika is in the most danger here. Wait...where is she? Does anyone know where Danika is?" Isaac questions.

"Now that you mention it, I don't recall seeing her when we gathered in the library before midnight. Actually, the last I remember seeing her was when she was greeting our guests," Matilda says with a hint of panic.

"I cannot reach her. I do not sense her anywhere near us. She must be far if I am not able to link with her mind," Alexander confirms.

"You don't think....?" Florence begins to panic.

Once again that girl is driving me batty. We need to find her and begin our training, to ensure our battle is won and Wenham remains safe forever. We finally have a life and I intend on living it to the fullest, for as long as I can. After more than a century, I have found friendship, and love. I have found my other half and am finally complete.

Charlotte Blackwell

Coming September 2011
Book Two of the Embrace Series
Forbidden Embrace

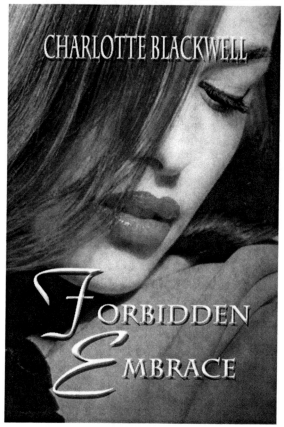

Sneak Preview

Forbidden Embrace

Chapter One
Clubbing

I decide to do a quick journal entry before leaving for the big New Year's party at Club VC. It has been a very eventful week. I have been spotted by at least two of my former family members. While doing a checkup on my family, I noticed Danika, the newest member of the family, conversing with a member of the Cerberus. They were making plans to celebrate the New Year at Club VC together. Young Danika still remains unaware of who she is dealing with. It appears the family is unaware of her power to block others. This is how Danika is able to keep her secrets. This is only a little tidbit I learned at the club. I'm not even sure if she is aware of her power yet.

I am concerned about Sophia seeing me in the park a little more than a week ago. I know that girl. She is as stubborn as a mule, and she will not give up on me. I need to be more careful now that Sophia is aware of my presence. I am sure she has divulged the information to the family by now. I expect her to look for me.

It's getting late. I should get ready and head for the club, in case Danika does go there. I want to keep an eye on her and keep her out of too much trouble. I have been attempting to disguise myself so Danika will not recognize me from pictures and the Cerberus will not recognize me if they have seen me around.

◆ ◆ ◆

Walking into the club, I look around for familiar faces– either Danika or the guy she has been meeting with. I find a few of the cult members I met during my previous visit here.

"Hey, Caspian. It's nice to see you back here," greets Cyrus.

I look at the older vampire who had welcomed me nights earlier. "Hi, Cyrus. Thanks. It is good to be back. Please call my Cas. I feel so free here, no hiding," I respond with little truth.

"Are you up for a drink?" He points to the bar.

"Sure. That's why I am here. I am always up for a little fun."

He leads me through the thick crowd of dancing vampires to the pounding tunes blaring from the speakers. Hundreds of rebellious vampires fill the club; some appear to be fresh out of the wastelands. I notice cages occupied by very attractive young vampires, scantily dressed. Tight leather and small tops appear to be the ensemble of choice. I could never understand how women can walk in heels that high. Many of the patrons are very interesting to look at, especially the ones with crazy hairstyles in an array of odd and unnatural colors. I start to think how much fun the club seems to be. Unfortunately, I know what types of vampires the owners are.

"You wanna tap or shot?" Cyrus asks when we reach the bar.

I look at the bar and see a young woman lying there. The vampires walk up to her and bite her in various spots, enjoying a drink from the poor soul that is barely alive.

"Let's try a shot," I respond, attempting to remain collected.

"Hey bartender, two shots please!" Cyrus shouts.

The bartender turns to the back of the bar, where a man lies motionless except for the shallow breathing movements of his chest. There is a type of intravenous needle in his carotid artery. The bartender grabs two shot glass in one hand and holds them to the needle cap. He opens the cap and drains the man's blood into the glasses, which he then hands to us. "Here you go boys. Enjoy."

"Cheers!" We clang glasses and take the shot.

I can't help but wonder what happens to the "donors." "I have to ask, how on Earth do you get the donors, and what do you do with them once they are drained?"

"We find transients, homeless people, addicts, and prostitutes. They are promised a good meal and a night of partying at a hot V.I.P club. Once we get them here, we clean them up and feed them. We use a sedative so they do not fight us. Some we Embrace, and others we throw back in the streets. The ones we Embrace become our cage dancers. This is our way of keeping control of them until they learn some discipline and won't get themselves destroyed," Cyrus explains. "You should go mingle with some of the others a little. We are always looking for new members that have eternal experience."

"Thank you. I will," I reply before I begin to roam the club.

I continue to look around and inspect the place. I did not get to see much last time I was here, so tonight is the time to familiarize myself. As I look up to the balconies above, I see

Danika, the little brat. She is with the same vampire that has been trying so hard to recruit her. It looks as if the upstairs area is where the top cult members party. Even with my impeccable hearing, I cannot zone in on what they are talking about over the crowd and music. I need to find a way to get invited upstairs. At least now I know where she is so I can keep an eye on her for my family's sake.

◆ ◆ ◆

Danika has been here for a while now, and I continue to mingle as I keep a watchful eye on her. I notice her walking down the stairs and decide to test my disguise. I walk toward her and advertently collide with her, making it look like an accident. "Oh! Please excuse me."

"No worries. My name is Danika, this is my first time here," she replies, proving she does not recognize me.

"Nice to meet you. I am Cas."

"Well, Cas, I hope to see you again. It is time for me to leave. I have a little travel ahead of me," she explains.

"I understand. Sunrise will be upon us soon. I think they'll be clearing the place out soon. Have a great rest. Maybe we will run into each other again," I say as we both leave the club.

Raised in Edmonton, Alberta, Charlotte enjoyed swimming, singing (although not so great at it) and writing her thoughts down. She never shared her passion for writing with anyone, and it got put on the back burner. As Charlotte grew, she found a new passion in medicine; she became the athletic trainer for her high school men's basketball team. Helping the team through their injuries are some of her best memories as a teen.

Charlotte has a strong passion for young adult novel especially those in the paranormal or dark fantasy genres.
http://charlotteblackwell.blogspot.com/

Charlotte Blackwell

272

Look for the next two releases in the Embrace Series

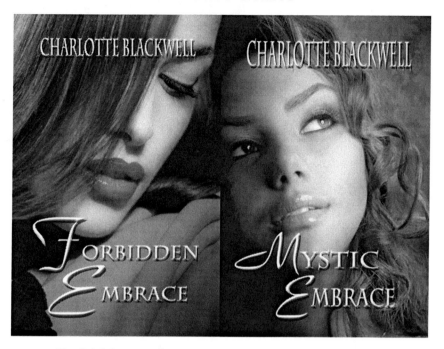

Forbidden Embrace	Mystic Embrace
September 1, 2011	November 1, 2011

CPSIA information can be obtained at www.ICGtesting.com
Printed in the USA
245056LV00011B/4/P